Forbidden Embrace

Embrace Series Book 2

Charlotte Blackwell

ISBN: 978-1-9993924-3-7

Library of Congress Catalogue Number 2011931980 (First edition)

First Edition World Castle Publishing September 1, 2011

Second Edition revised and re-released by JSLB Publishing July 2018

Licensing Notes

Cover Artist: CJ Strange

Dedication

To my wonderful family, friends, and readers that have all supported and encouraged me through this process. Thank you and I love you all; because of your support I have found myself and what I truly love to do.
This is for all the vampire lovers of the world because only a vampire can love you forever.

Contents

Chapter 1

Caspian Club VC

A quick journal entry seems wise before I leave for the big New Year's party at Club VC. It's been an eventful week; I've been spotted by at least two of my estranged family members. While doing a checkup on my family, I noticed Danika, the newest member of the family, conversing with a member of the Cerberus, making plans to celebrate the New Year at Club VC together. Young Danika remains unaware of who she's dealing with, and it appears the family is unaware of her power to block others. This is how Danika's able to keep her secrets. This is only a little tidbit I learned at the club; I'm not even sure if she's aware of her power yet.

I'm concerned about Sophia seeing me in the park a little more than a week ago. I know that girl. She's as stubborn as a mule and won't give up on me. I need to be more careful now that She's aware of my presence. I'm sure she divulged the information to the family by now. I expect her to be looking for me.

It's getting late; I should get ready and head for the club, in case Danika does go there. I want to keep an eye on her and keep her out of too much trouble. I've been attempting to disguise myself, so

Danika won't recognize me from pictures, and the Cerberus won't recognize me if they see me away from the club.

∞ ∞ ∞

Walking into the club, I look around for familiar faces, either Danika or the guy she's been meeting with. I find a few of the cult members I met during my previous visit here.

"Hey, Caspian. It's nice to see you back here," greets Cyrus.

I look at the older vampire who'd welcomed me a few nights earlier. "Hi, Cyrus. Thanks. It is good to be back. Please call me Cas. I feel so free here…no hiding, time to let loose." I respond with little truth.

"You up for a drink?" he points to the bar.

"Sure. That's why I'm here. I'm always up for a little fun."

He leads me through the thick crowd of vampires dancing to the pounding tunes blaring from the speakers. Hundreds of rebellious vampires fill the club; some appear to be fresh out of the wastes. I notice cages occupied by very attractive young vampires, scantily dressed. Tight leather and small tops appear to be the ensemble of choice paired with high heels. I'll never understand how women can walk in heels that high, they must be at least four inches; although it does make their legs look very nice, shapely and luxurious. Even in the eternal life women can be so vain; every little detail must be perfect. Many have to look their best no matter the cost. I personally prefer a more natural look. Many of the patrons are very interesting to look at, especially the ones with crazy hairstyles in an array of odd and unnatural colors. I start to think how much fun the club seems to be. Unfortunately, I know what type of vampires the owners are and what kind of guests they have here.

"You want a tap or shot?" Cyrus asks when we reach the bar.

I look at the bar and see a young woman lying there. Vampires walk up to her and bite her in various spots, enjoying a drink from the poor soul that's barely alive.

"Let's try a shot," I respond, attempting to remain collected. I can't deny that being around the fresh blood and even drinking it on occasion hasn't been tough, cause it's hard as hell. I need to keep up appearances for the club members though. I'll just have to detox after.

"Hey buddy, two shots please!" Cyrus shouts.

The bartender turns to the back of the bar, where a man lies motionless except for the shallow movements of his chest. There's a type of intravenous needle in his carotid artery. The bartender grabs two shot glasses in one hand and holds them to the needle cap. Opening the cap and draining an ounce of the man's blood into each glass, which he then hands to us. "Here you go, boys. Enjoy."

"Cheers!" We clang glasses and take the shot, turning the glasses upside down on the bar when done.

I can't help but wonder what happens to the 'donors.' "I have to ask, how on Earth do you get the donors, and what do you do with them once they are drained?"

"We find transients, homeless people, addicts, and prostitutes. They are promised a good meal and a night of partying at a hot V.I.P club. Once we get them here, we clean them up and feed them. We use a sedative, so they don't fight us. Some we Embrace, and others we throw back in the streets. The ones we Embrace become our cage dancers. This is our way of keeping control of them until they learn some discipline and won't get themselves destroyed," Cyrus explains. "You should go mingle with some of the others a little. We are always looking for new members that have some eternal experience."

"Thanks, I will," I reply before I begin to roam the club.

I continue to look around and inspect the place, taking various mental notes. I didn't get to see much last time I was here; tonight's the time to familiarize myself. As I look up to the balconies above, I see Danika; the little brat. She's with the same vampire that's been trying so hard to recruit her. It looks as if the upstairs area is where the top cult members party. Even with my impeccable hearing, I can't zone in on what they're talking about over the crowd and music. I need to find a way to get invited upstairs. At least now I know where she is, so I can keep an eye on her for my family's sake.

∞ ∞ ∞

Danika's been here for a while now, and I continue to mingle as I keep a watchful eye on her. I notice her walking down the stairs and decide to test my disguise, so I walk toward her and advertently collide with her, making it look like an accident. "Oh! Please excuse me."

"No worries. I'm Danika, it's my first time here," she replies, proving she doesn't recognize me.

"Nice to meet you. I'm Cas."

"Well, Cas, I hope to see you again. It's time for me to leave. I gotta get home before my family notices I snuck out," she explains.

"I understand. Sunrise will be upon us soon anyway. I think they'll be clearing the place out soon. Maybe we'll run into one another again," I say as we both leave the club.

It's been difficult hiding from my family…thirty years on the run is too long, even when you have eternity. I can only hope they forgive me for draining and killing my girlfriend Ashley. Maybe one day I can forgive myself as well. After it happened, I just couldn't face them and had to leave. I didn't deserve to be a part of their family; I'd failed them all. But I've always kept a close eye on my estranged family and it's finally paying off. I'm hoping to prove to them that I can handle my bloodlust. If I can help protect them against the Cerberus, the rogue vampire cult that's been scoping out the area, they may forgive me and let me have another chance. Last year when they, the Pierces', moved back to Wenham, Massachusetts, they never expected to fight with some of the most dangerous of our kind, the Cerberus. The area's supernaturally charged; the magic from the area can attract evil of all kinds, seeking more power. The rich magical history is leading the Cerberus directly to them. Now if I can only help steer Danika, the newest vampire in the Pierce family, in the right direction, I'll be able to move on to more important matters. Protecting and regaining my place in the Pierce family is the only thing that matters to me.

Chapter 2

Worry

I just knew it! I knew Danika would be trouble! This is going to be bad for each and every one of us. I should've stuck with my initial instinct about her. I wonder if anyone went missing from the New Year's party? We're all having so much fun getting to know more of the town's people, and now this. If she kills some innocent party guest, I'll destroy her myself. If she leaves them alive and is unable to compel them properly, we'll be discovered. I'm going to beat the crap out of that little brat, I think as I pace the room in frustration.

"We'll find her and deal with the ramifications of her actions. Then we'll deal with the Cerberus. I don't want anyone to jump to conclusions." Elijah looks directly at me with his eyebrows raised, knowing that I have already done so.

"I agree, a member of our family is missing, and danger is heading this way. We'll feed and then go look for Danika. At this point we don't know what's happening; all we know is that she's missing," Isaac points out.

It’s nearly four in the morning, and we still don’t know where Danika is. Florence prepares something for us to eat before we go and try to find her. None of us enjoy the meal Florence prepared, as we’re all too worried about what’s to come. We decide it’s best just to go now and search for Danika, but at that same moment, we notice her walking up the drive towards the house.

Opening the front door, my rage takes over. “Are you freaking kidding me? You take off without telling anyone and just walk up the drive like nothing even happened?!” I scream.

“Look, I'm sorry; I should’ve left a note or told someone I needed to get out of here. It was just too much for me to handle,” Danika defends.

“Danika, I'm sorry, but if the party was difficult for you, you should’ve come and talked to one of us. That’s what we're here for…that’s what family is for,” Florence says as she opens her arms and wraps them around Danika.

“I'm really sorry to worry you. I’m not used to having anyone care about me. I really didn't think anyone would notice I was gone. If you don't mind though, I'd really like to take a shower. Can we talk more about it tomorrow maybe?” She tucks a strand of hair from her short red hair behind her ear, looking at us with childlike eyes.

“Can you at least tell us where you were Danika?” Elijah questions.

“I was just exploring the woods; I needed to get away and be by myself.”

“We’ll talk about this tomorrow. I think we all need to get some rest. We have a lot to talk about in the days to come,” Elijah insists. It is obvious that the upcoming threat is weighing heavily on him.

∞ ∞ ∞

I'm restless and want nothing more than to wring that girl's neck. Pacing back and forth in my room, my anger continues to consume me. I always knew she'd be trouble, but I never thought it'd be this bad. How can she do this to us, after everything our family has done for her? What a selfish little brat to put our secret, our family, in danger like that. Something could've happened; someone could have seen her. That girl thinks about nothing but herself and she needs to smarten up before she brings all of us down with her. I've had a bad feeling about her since the first day, eighteen months ago. The only good thing is that because of her forcing me to return to school that I met my soul mate Nathanial and my best friend Ebony, a young witch. I guess I can be grateful for that.

With a knock at my door, Alexander asks, "Can I come in?"

"Of course," I answer.

He sits next to me on the bed. "I can't help but hear you freaking out about Danika. It's not as bad as you're making it out to be. Don't you remember what it was like when we first became vampires?" Alexander tries to calm me.

"We were nowhere as irresponsible as she is being," I argue.

"Really? Maybe you just don't realize, since we were in the middle of nowhere and then we're on our mission to find Miss Edwina and her mother. We were preoccupied."

I can't even imagine where we would be without Miss Edwina, a powerful witch of Salem descent. When Miss Edwina and her mother blessed our day crystals, our lives changed forever. I don't want this brat of a little sister to ruin it all.

"I still have a bad feeling about her. I just know she's up to something."

"Okay, I understand that, but with the news, we received today maybe we should focus on more important issues."

I acknowledge this with a sigh. "I guess you're right. We need to deal with the Cerberus, which is definitely a bigger threat than a teenage vampire." *Or are they,* I wonder?

Thankfully the Renata, the leaders of vampires, or at least the more civilized vampires and have vowed to assist us.

"So please calm down; we'll find out more tomorrow about what happened with Danika and then we plan for the Cerberus. I'm always here for you and hate seeing you so distressed." Alexander leans over and hugs me before leaving.

Alexander's right; I need to calm down. Maybe I'll work on my scrapbooking a little. I have so many wonderful memories to document. I still can't believe how blessed I've become. After Caspian, left the family, I was torn. Wenham has brought me a new-found happiness and meaning. Now that I know Caspian is lurking around, I'm hopeful he'll return to us.

Chapter 3

Details

Morning comes, and of course, Danika offers no more explanations for us. Elijah makes sure that the entire family understands the ramifications of our actions with a true fatherly lecture. Then announces it's time to move past Danika's disappearance and time to begin work on stopping the Cerberus.

"I'm going to spend the day with Nathanial. I think I need to do some explaining to him and prepare him for what's coming," I announce, nervously picking at my nails.

"That's a good idea. Do you need some backup?" Alexander asks, with a wink.

"Thanks, I think I'd rather do this on my own. Stay here and help Elijah, there's a lot to prepare for."

Alexander agrees, and the men head to the office as I grab my coat. Nathanial pulls up in perfect time.

We decide to disappear for the day, so we drive up the mountain to a spot I found when my family and I were out scouting animals. It's beautiful, open yet secluded, surrounded by trees centuries old and a beautiful waterfall slowed by winter freeze. We park and begin to walk the little hiking path and make our way up the old style wooden staircase up the hill. I imagine the area full of wildflowers in the summer with the sun shimmering through the trees.

This place reminds me of young families hiking to their favorite picnic spot. I picture the mother setting up their lunch as the children frolic in the area. I even imagine Nathanial and I in this spot with our children, although I know having children with Nathanial isn't an option; but it's a beautiful daydream. Sometimes dreams are all I have.

It 's relaxing, I enjoy our surroundings; the light trickle of the almost frozen waterfall is so relaxing, and the sound of small animals scurrying through the thickened brush is peaceful. On the cold hard ground, ice flecks glisten in the sun. As I look around I realize this is the true beauty the world has to offer. But we're here for a reason; I need to explain more to Nathanial and tell him the ugly truth about my world.

Nathanial needs more details about me, my existence and what's to come.

"This place is wonderful!" He gives me one of those crooked half smiles and runs his hand through his truffle brown hair in the way that makes me melt.

"I know. We found it one night when we were looking for food," I explain. "I figure now would be a good time to explain everything to you."

"Fantastic. I want to know it all."

"Well I'll begin with a little vampire history; what do you know about vampires? Actually, never mind, I'll just explain if that's okay," I mutter, nervously tapping my foot.

"Relax, you don't need to be nervous. I'm not going to judge you; just explain and I'll listen, saving all questions for after your explanation." He soothes me within seconds.

"Fair enough but stop me if it becomes too much for you to handle," I insist.

"From the beginning, there's been a legend that the first of our kind was Cain, the son of Adam and the first murderer. Cain murdered his brother Abel because God preferred the gifts Abel gave to him over Cain's gifts. It was out of pure jealousy that Cain killed his brother. God couldn't believe Cain had done such a thing, and as punishment, Cain was cursed by God, forced to walk the earth alone night after night for all eternity. Cain was exiled from the people and forced to stalk civilization. He feared the sun because it burned him and was extremely painful. He'd come out at night to hunt the mortals; he was ravenous for blood." I begin to pace a little.

"Cain met a powerful witch named Lilith, who some believe to be Adam's first wife. I personally don't understand how that could be possible. I mean if you believe in God, don't you believe that Adam and Eve were the first humans created? If that's true, how was Lilith his first wife?"

"Sophia, you're rambling," Nathanial chuckles.

"Sorry, right. Okay, so Lilith has also been called the goddess of night, a demon and the bearer of disease, illness, and death. She showed Cain how to use his own blood for magic and evoke his unknown mystical powers. This is how he became the first vampire. From Lilith, Cain learned how to create others of his kind. This is called 'Embracing'…a mortal must be bitten by a vampire, then the venom or poison in their saliva combined with a few drops of the vampire's own blood begins the transformation. The mortal body ceases and the immortal body takes over. Now, this can only happen as long as the mortal isn't drained of too much blood–there must be enough to keep the heart beating. The vampire blood and venom enters the mortal's system as the heart pumps it through the entire body, and the Embrace begins."

I pause for a moment to gauge his reaction, which is nothing except complete and intense interest, so I continue with the story.

"The full process can take hours or weeks, depending on conditions of the mortal body. Illness, broken bones, anything that ailed the mortal body begins to repair and heal. The heartbeat slows, and breathing is no longer much of a necessity as less oxygen is needed. The immortal must learn to use their new gifts, speed, strength, increased senses. A vampire needs very little sleep; although once they achieve fulfillment in their eternal lives a vampire will actually sleep more than they need, mortal food makes a vampire feel ill, and a thirst for blood increases." I sigh and gather my thoughts. "Is this helping at all?" I ask Nathanial.

"This is the most interesting story I have ever heard, please continue."

"Okay, well some of the other changes that the new vampire goes through include paling of the skin and feeling cold to the touch, both caused because of decreased blood flow in the body. Blood continues to circulate, just at a much slower rate and with less pressure than a mortal. The new vampire becomes feather light on their feet, and they have extreme photosensitivity. The increased senses include super hearing and sight, increased sense of smell and taste, and increased feeling or sense of touch. A vampire exudes sex appeal and an increased release of pheromones. This helps to attract mortals. Even the rogue vampires that live underground, who aren't particularly physically attractive, have extreme sex appeal. " I smile, and Nathanial leans over and gently kisses me.

With a small smile I carry on, "A vampire's powers include, but are not limited to, creating others, extreme jumping almost to the point of flying, climbing or scaling, and swimming long distances; although, crossing moving water can be difficult, but there are always ways to get around it. Vampires can't regenerate lost limbs but can reattach them; cuts and small breaks heal within moments, large breaks in days. There's also the power of persuasion or compulsion, hypnosis, and of course eternal life. Now, as you already know, there's also separate powers that can be different or are unique to the individual."

"If the heart slows can a vampire still bleed?"

"Yes. But it doesn't flow as freely as a living creature. Our blood is also the deepest red you can imagine…almost black. Not to mention healing makes the clotting happen almost instantly."

"I guess the flow makes sense, but red blood? I thought the blood became red when oxygenated, and if you don't need to breathe as much how does that work?"

"Well, we do still need to breathe, just not as much. A vampire's body is much more efficient than a mortal's; honestly, there are just some things that are unexplainable, and our blood and bodily functions are some of them. The most unexplainable vampire fact is our immortality and how we cease aging. There's lots about us that can't be explain by biology or physics."

We both kinda chuckle and Nathanial nod.

"So, what happened to Cain?" Nathanial asks.

"Well, Cain became lonely and Embraced five others, to create his own family. These vampires ravaged the area, feeding carelessly, and used the mortals against one another. Outraged, Cain became frustrated and forbade them from creating any more vampires. Cain was said to have built the 'first city'. Once he was exiled from Eden, a place where vampires and mortals coexisted peacefully, the peace didn't last long. The younger vampires began fighting, believing they were better than the mortals. I assume this was the first case of racism." I smirk and continue, "They used the mortals for fun, killing uncontrollably, and the city was overthrown. Cain vanished, never to be heard from again, along with the three of the five vampires he created," I elucidate.

"The two children that stayed became reckless in creating new vampires and fifteen grandchildren to Cain forming clans. The clans fought each other for power and rule, and numbers reached crazy proportions. The mortals began to fight back. They would drag vampires one by one from their homes or lairs as they were called back then to burn in the sun. Once the vampire was weakened and burned enough, the people would tear the vampire apart and behead them, which ensured death to the immortal." I gaze at Nathanial and we smile at each other. He gives my hand a little squeeze, his eyes still wide with interest.

I carry on with the history lesson. "Around the fifth century, nine of the fifteen clans joined in an organization they called 'The Renata'. They suppressed the radicals and began their conspiracy of silence. They ruled that vampires shouldn't kill openly and should conceal their natures from the mortals. This began the great myth of vampires. The Renata created six Laws to be followed by all and to continue the conspiracy, laws that Cain would have seen fit to live civilly. The Laws are...

1st Law

The Conspiracy

Thou shall not reveal the nature of thy being to anyone.

2nd Law

The Empire

Thy Empire is thine own concern and no other shall interfere.

Only the leaders may intervene if rules are forsaken.

All others owe thee respect while in it.

3rd Law

The Ancestry

Thou shall only Embrace another with the permission of thy leader,

Until one's own Empire is formed, and one is released from thy leader.

4th Law

Accountability

Thou art responsible for thy creations; rule them in all things.

5th Law

Respectfulness

Honor one another's Empire.

Thou must be respectful to the ruler of another Empire.

6th Law

Destruction

Thou art forbidden to destroy another's Embraced;

The right belongs only to thy ruler.

The radicals who didn't join were driven into the wastes, and later the Cerberus cult emerged. The wars between the two groups continued for centuries, and still happen today. Now, as with any law, the six laws have been broken, bent and slightly changed to fit with the times. The sixth law has been altered to, 'thou may destroy another of thy kind to protect thine Empire'."

Nate interrupts, "This is so cool. So, it's kinda like the ten commandments? Does your family follow these 'Laws'?"

"Yeah, we do to a point. As you said they are kinda like the ten commandments and just like people choose to follow parts, we vampires are similar. They are fairly outdated."

"Where's this Renata located?"

"Okay, don't laugh, but they're from Transylvania. It's actually the first city that was rebuilt and now carries Cain's original vision of co-existence."

"Seriously? So like Dracula?"

"Yeah, actually he's one of Cain's grandsons."

"That's so freakin cool! Please go on."

"The newest of wars were the riots of New York in 1880's. By early 1900's the vampire population hit one million worldwide. Now, here is a quick rundown of vampire history in the government. In 1943 President Franklin D. Roosevelt unveiled a special task force and project. The government created a vaccine to fight against the millennia of vampire activity. In 1950 a man in New Mexico was given the first vampire vaccine. The new vaccine was able to weaken the virus but wasn't able to simulate the antibodies to protect against it. The USA and the Soviets began testing the blood, believing that immortality was in the DNA. In 1967 the United Nations placed a ban on vampire blood testing. In 1986 President Reagan lifted the ban on this testing and research. Things have been fairly calm for the last few decades, until two days ago when Constance had a vision."

"What kind of vision do you mean?" Nathanial asks.

“I guess I should just spit it out; the Cerberus has risen from the wastes of New York. They are on a killing spree and heading our way.” I ramble this out fast, just to get it over with. I feel a sense of relief by sharing, although I can see the concern in his eyes.

“Okay, wait a second; dangerous vampires are headed this way? How concerned should I be, and do you know what they want?”

“Well I’m not quite sure yet, but we’ll know more once we talk to Elijah. He’s in contact with the Renata and my family is working hard to try and figure things out. I’ll tell you what I know once I explain a little more. Are you okay?”

“Not quite sure yet? This is a little more than scary. I guess we just have to see what the plan is once we get back to your place. What else can you tell me?”

“Well, that is the cliff notes version of vampire history. Would you like to hear about my family history next?”

“Yeah, I do. I’m just shocked that the American government knows about all this! I would not be surprised anymore if you told me area 51 is real,” he jokes.

“Well, aliens are real if that’s what you mean,” I laugh. “And most members of the government don’t know all of this to be truth; only a select few know of the supernatural. They like the majority of elected officials and public to believe it to be myth.”

“So, vampires, witches, aliens…what else is real?” Nathanial questions with a bit of shock.

“I’m really just kidding about the aliens…that I don’t know about. But yes, vampires, witches, and werewolves, banshees, angels, demons, wizards, and warlocks; those kinds of creatures all exist along with many others.”

“Okay, well,” he lets out a sigh, “will you tell me about your family now? I’ll let all that sink in later.” He smiles and squeezes my hand.

And so, I begin again. “I was born Sophia Suvanto, on October seventeenth, 1876. I was the oldest of three girls and my twin brother Alex was the only son; my family were socialites in Italy, considered a low-ranking royalty. Although extremely privileged, I was expected to marry up the social ladder; my family was all about social advancement. My hand had been promised to a suitor, a Duke I’d only met once, and he was fifteen years my senior. I was extremely unhappy about the arrangement; I wanted more, and I wanted love, but I was bound by duty to my family.” Knowing I've finally found the love I was looking for, I glance over at Nathanial and smile. “I decided to go for a walk one evening to clear my head and focus on the task at hand. I walked the streets of my town in Italy, but I took a wrong turn and ended up down an alley I didn’t know. It was very dark, almost eleven o’clock at night. I felt an unsettling presence behind me, and before I could run someone grabbed me. He began twisting my arm behind my back, shattering almost every bone. I screamed in agony. He beat me, and then bit my neck and began to drink the blood pouring out of my wound. He was having fun and laughing as if it were a game to him. I heard footsteps running toward the alley.” I shudder at the memory.

“My attacker left and hid in the shadows before the footsteps reached me. The footsteps I had heard were Alexander’s; he’d come to my rescue. Alex tried to control the bleeding and screamed to the man he saw at the other end of the alley for help. What he didn’t know is that man was not a man; he was a monster. I tried to warn him but couldn't speak. It was the same monster that had attacked me, and he then attacked Alex," I continue to explain, just as Alexander did when showing Ebony and her sister with his telepathic powers.

"So, you and Alex are not only twins by birth, but also by the day you became vampires?" Nathanial asks.

"Yes, we're both birth and immortal twins. I think it's kinda the irony of the whole situation. Alex didn't even realize it was me at first. We entered the world together and entered eternity together. We were both Embraced by Elijah's clan on the same day. It's Alex's kind heart that made him a vampire. He thought he was helping some strange girl and would have done it for anyone. Alex and I were left for dead, barely hanging on. Constance had a vision of us, and that is what led their clan to us. From that moment on Alex and I were considered missing persons; our bodies were never found. It was August seventh, 1894, shortly before our eighteenth birthday and my upcoming nuptials. This is when we became immortal."

I can see Nathanial getting very upset; I sense the fury raging within him. "Are you okay?" I ask.

"I will be; it's just hearing of someone…something doing that to you for fun…I just wish I could get my hands on him!" he rages.

"No need, Elijah already took care of him," I reassure. "From that moment on we became the Pierce family. Is this helping you to understand?" I ask.

"I enjoy learning about you, though I don't enjoy hearing of the suffering you endured before becoming a vampire," he says and hugs me, holding me tighter than ever before. "Can you tell me about Ebony and her family?" he requests.

"I'll tell you more about our family and Ebony's a little later," I insist. "I'd like to tell you more about the vision Constance had the other night…it is fairly important," I add.

"What is it? You seem so serious; is everything alright?" He appears very concerned now but tries to comfort me. He rubs the back of my neck and looks deeply into my eyes.

"As I mentioned earlier, on New Year's Eve Constance had a vision. She saw the Cerberus cult rising from the wastes of New York. There's been several murders in New York lately. The police believe it to be a serial killer, but Constance envisioned the Cerberus being responsible, and they are on their way to the New England area."

"Do I need to tell my family to leave?" he asks.

"Well, we're working on a plan to keep the entire town safe," I ensure.

"The Cerberus knows about the history of the area and the mystical powers around here. The Cerberus cult wants to collect powers and build an army of sorts. Their plan, as Constance saw it, is to challenge the Renata for ruling power. Elijah contacted the Renata and our family is preparing for battle; they've entrusted us to handle the matter," I explain.

"What do you mean 'handle it'?"

I can see his concern growing even more, as he begins to wring his hands together.

"Could people from here get hurt? Could you get hurt?"

"We all could, but we aren't going to let that happen," I reassure.

"I want to be involved," he insists.

“Absolutely not! I'll agree to have you in the know, but you will not be anywhere in sight when the fight happens. You could get killed…it’s way too dangerous,” I argue.

“You don’t want me around because it’s is too dangerous, but what you don’t realize is that I don’t want you to be in danger either,” he disputes.

“Okay, I see your point, but I’m immortal. I won’t get hurt,” I persist.

“Wow. Pretty intense. We’ll see what happens, but I want to know everything, full disclosure,” he demands, and I agree.

“I want to warn you that the Renata won’t be happy if they find out about us telling you our secret. It breaks the first law. They could destroy my family and you as well. We must be very careful,” I say with a hint of fear.

“What about Ebony and her family?” Nathanial wonders.

“They’re fine; the law has been modified to include others of supernatural decent.”

“Okay, so we’ll have to be careful now that the Renata is involved.”

“Yes, you can’t let on that you know anything. My family will have to behave even more human when you’re around. Most of all we’ve got to try to conceal our relationship. If anything, I have to make it appear as though I am scouting you to join because you have something to offer. What worries me about that is they may make it happen if we’re not careful. Do you understand?”

“Yes. Please calm down…everything will work out! Just so I am clear, you’re worried that they may ‘Embrace’ me, as you call it. My question is, what’s so wrong with that? I realize I promised you I wouldn’t bring it up, but I would be honored,” Nathanial admits.

"Honored? There's nothing honorable about becoming a vampire. For more than a hundred years I've felt trapped, stuck in a teenager's body and all alone. Everyone else in my family has someone to share their eternity with, and even though I have you now I want you to have everything I never did and never will. I just won't allow that to happen! You don't know what you are asking for; it just isn't an option, so you can stop asking and hinting!" I start to get upset now. I love Nathanial for who he is and don't want to do anything to change it or him.

"I'm sorry; I didn't mean to upset you. I won't bring it up again," he says, very apologetically.

"Thank you, I don't mean to get so upset over it; this is just not a life I wish for someone I love," I insist. We both forget about it and continue to enjoy the surroundings. We agree to the terms of his non-involvement in the fight. I understand what he's been going through, but I just can't handle the idea of taking everything away from him.

I love him so much, I just want to enjoy the time I have with him. Now he's learning everything about me and my family, I hope he'll still accept it all. There I go, over analyzing things again. I worry way too much and just need to accept that Nathanial loves me!

"I don't want to argue with you. I have such a sense of relief that you are learning everything about me and would really love to enjoy this moment."

"I agree, Sweetie, this is a pivotal moment in our relationship, and we should enjoy it." Nathanial grabs me and holds me in his arms with love and admiration.

Chapter 4

Preparations

Nathanial and I return to the house shortly before five o'clock. Florence has prepared a little dinner for Nathanial, and I join him just because Florence is such a good cook and I don't want him to feel uncomfortable eating alone. Elijah's been hard at work, hammering out details and creating a plan with the Renata. They're sending someone to track the Cerberus, so we can be better prepared. Once they get close enough we'll attack and destroy them. Isaac explains the plan to Nathanial and I.

"We're going to have to start some physical training. It's been a long time since we have had to use our strength and endurance. This isn't going to be easy–we don't know how many there will be, nor do we know their strengths," Isaac informs us.

"Do we know if they are Embracing any others? Newer vampires will be easier to beat, and we can deplete the numbers before going for the stronger ones," Alexander asks.

"We can only assume that they are. There's been reports of missing people from the area. We just have no idea of what their numbers are," Isaac confirms.

"All of you have to fight? What can I do to help?" Nathanial inquires.

"Nothing! You can stay far away from all this," I shout.

"Sophia's right, Nate…this is too dangerous for you. They can and will destroy you, which in turn will destroy Sophia. You don't want to hurt her, right?" Florence interjects.

"No, I don't, but I also don't want her fighting," he insists.

"We all need to be there; we're stronger as a family," Florence tries to console him. "Of course, there is one exception; Danika. She is too new."

"What?" The surprise is written all over her face.

"Danika, we need your help elsewhere. You need to ensure the McCord's remain safe, which in turn will keep you safe," Constance adds, and Danika nods in agreement. She always seems to listen to Constance.

"We have the most powerful help to protect us. I went to see Ebony and her sister today. They're going to fight with us. They're the most powerful beings on Earth when they work together. The Magnificent Ones are already preparing potions and spells. Eliza's researching their Book of Shadows for more information," Alexander explains.

"Nate, I'll be fine, I promise, we talked about this already." I hold his hand in mine. "I just need to know that you're safe; I can't worry about you during all of this," I tell him.

"Fine, but as we agreed, I want to be involved in all the planning and details. I want to know what is happening and what the risks are. I also want to know when you're going. I expect full disclosure in all things related to this matter. This is non-negotiable."

I can see his frustration. “I agreed to this earlier and will honor my word.” We seal our agreement with a kiss.

“Okay, I think Nate’s had enough to deal with for one day. Can we take the evening off from fight detail?” I request.

“Yes, I think you two should do something fun for the evening,” Constance urges.

“How about bowling? It would be a great way to get our minds off things. Mati and Alex can come,” I suggest.

“That sounds great,” Matilda answers.

“Bowling it is. Why don’t we call Ebony, Matt, and Eliza? We could go get Luke; he’s got it bad for Eliza,” Nathanial recommends.

We drive by the McCord house and grab Luke. Ebony, Matt, and Eliza meet us at the bowling alley. I don’t know Luke very well, but it is so funny....he’s absolutely enamored with Eliza. Nathanial and I enjoy watching them together…they just get lost when the other is around. It’s really too bad that he has to go back to school in the next day or so.

It’s nice to relax and just enjoy our time together with friends. The plan is to spend a few hours there, munch on some appetizers and drink sodas. We Pierce kids want to keep up the façade, so we plan to join the others for some snacks.

“Why don’t we get a few competitions going on; couples pitted against couples, battle of the sexes and so on?” Luke suggests. “Why didn’t Danika come tonight? She seems like a good kid.”

“HA! Seriously, she’s trouble. She stayed at home. We thought it would be nice to have a couple’s night,” I laugh.

“Sophia doesn’t care for our little sister too much. You know how it goes, sibling rivalry and all. Danika looks up to Sophia so much and Sophia is just a bag of teenage hormones,” Alexander chuckles.

I take a swing at him. "Oh, bite me Alex; watch it or you will be the next sibling on my hit list."

"Break it up you two. Let's just accept that Sophia doesn't like her little sister and forget about it. I thought we came here for some fun," Nathanial insists.

Everyone agrees, and we set up our teams. We agree to leave powers and strengths at the door when Luke excuses himself to the men's room. With all the giggling and friendly banter, I realize that I haven't had so much fun in ages. We've really found our place here in Wenham, and I'll really hate to leave it one day. This is exactly what I need, to feel normal and be with friends. What a perfect start to a new year; at least for now.

∞ ∞ ∞

When we get home, it's late and time for Nathanial to head back to his place. The entire family comes out to say goodnight.

"Thank you for explaining so much to me today. It's nice to know more about you, and I'm glad that you and your family trust me with all this knowledge."

"I hope I didn't completely overwhelm you. We have so much time for me to tell you more, but I wanted to explain about myself, and the threat that is approaching."

"Don't worry about me, I'm fine; just wish I'd brought a notepad," he jokes. I give him a playful punch in the arm. "Ouch," he yelps.

"Sorry, sorry! I didn't mean...."

"I'm just kidding sweetie."

"Careful or next time I will hurt you."

He leans in and gives me a kiss goodnight. “Have a good night sweetie, I love you.”

“I love you too,” I reply with my arms still tightly wrapped over his broad shoulders.

I watch as he jumps back in his car and drives away. I still can’t believe that after so many years I’ve finally found the love I always wished for. Once inside I start pacing, the worry of how he’ll feel after it all settles.

“What is it, Sophia?” Alexander asks.

“I’m really worried about Nate tonight. It’s a lot of information for him to take in. I try not to worry but I can’t help it; I’m a Libra and it is one of my main traits. I think I’ll sneak over and check on him tonight. I just want to ensure he’s alright with all the insight into our existence.”

“Have you forgotten, I’m a Libra too, not to mention we are twins? I am quite aware of all your traits.”

Inside my family’s discussing everything the Renata has told Elijah about the Cerberus cult of New York. From what they know there are about ten vampires involved, not including any new members they create. With the seven of us and the three witches, Ebony, Eliza, and their Grams we’ll be even, not counting the new vampires. They won’t have the strength or skill to fight us, so they’ll just be pawns to distract us.

Matilda explains that Ebony and Eliza are going into Boston to the Wicca/New age store. They plan to stock up on everything they may need for potions. Herbs, roots, bottles, dried insects and magic crystals will all be of aid. Eliza will also get some gemstones for spells and for scrying.

“What’s scrying?” I ask.

"Scrying is a process used by witches to find someone or something. It will be our way of keeping track of everybody if for some reason we become separated," Eliza explains.

"We also want to cover all of us with protection spells, since the ones for Matt and Nate worked so well. We'll need to test that because we're not sure how the protection spells will affect our powers or abilities. We already know they work since Eliza tested the boys before Christmas. We have a lot of work to do over the next few days," Ebony adds.

I'm even more happy that Ebony and I got the boys gifts to protect them from the supernatural; she gave Matt a wristband and I gave Nathanial a watch. Eliza and Ebony, along with the help of their Grams, Ms. Edwina, placed a protection spell on the gifts. Thankfully they have them for when the Cerberus arrive.

"We need to be well fed at all times, not allowing any weakness. We need a plan to go scouting on a daily basis to ensure fresh blood is used. I also think that we should find human donors since fresh human blood makes us the strongest. We can't go too late because the Cerberus can't come out in the day, so we want to be prepared for the nightfall when they come out. Tomorrow we start physical training." Elijah explains.

"Did you say fresh human blood? What about our vow to not hurt others?" The nervousness of the situation comes out as I speak.

"Yes, Sophia, I know it's going to be difficult for all of us. We're used to the donated human blood we've been feeding with, but the fresher it is the better. We've discussed things and have a few thoughts about how to go about getting fresh blood."

"What about Danika? There's no way that at only a year and a half she can handle fresh blood! I'm terrified at how the rest of us will cope, and you all know I don't trust her as it is."

"We've already decided that she'll remain on her usual diet, for everyone's protection, also because she will be with the McCord's, she won't need the same strength as us," he informs. "As for the rest of us, we will find willing live donors."

"Who the hell will that be? We need to still keep our cover. It's not like we can take an ad out in the Sunday paper."

"Very true my dear. When we were discussing our options our wonderful witch friends have offered to help by providing some for us. Another option is to practice our compelling skills. Using transients will be best. We can compensate them as well," Florence adds.

"Okay, you are telling me that Ebony and her family have offered us their blood? Not a chance, they're my friends, I will not bite any of them! Then the matter of using transients; what if they are drug users or have diseases? Won't their blood be tainted? Will that not affect us?"

"Have you completely lost all your senses, Sophia? We should all be able to smell a tainted vessel from miles away," Isaac snaps. "If using tainted blood is the only option, our bodies will repair from the disease. The only downfall is that uses energy, so it is better to avoid bad blood."

"Vessel?" Eliza questions.

Isaac chuckles and explains. "Sorry…old word for human, or the vessel for the blood."

"Okay. Yeah, I guess my emotions got the best of me. You've been talking about feeding off the only friends I've had in over a century. Yeah, just a little overwhelmed here," I say defensively.

“Sophia don’t worry about it. You and your family need fresh blood to ensure your strength. The good news is I have lots of it. Isaac explained that it will not be much and never by a bite. He’ll use his medical equipment. This will prevent the spread of venom in our system. We’ll be fine.” Ebony is very convincing. “Our magical blood should enhance you in other ways as well, like making your own powers stronger.”

“Okay, but won’t the blood loss weaken you?”

“We will only use minimal amounts and during the day, so they can replenish before nightfall,” Isaac assures.

I sit down in the family room in an attempt to process the plan. I need to ensure my mind has full mental clarity. With a few calming moments, I agree. We can’t protect this town and its people that have come to mean so much to us if we’re weakened. Drinking fresh human blood is the only way we can win this fight.

We finish deciding how to go about things, the feeding, the fight and so on. I figure now is the time to check up on Nathanial. I want Alexander to come with me, but not to be seen. I’m hoping that Alexander can get into Nathanial’s subconscious and ensure me that all is copasetic.

Chapter 5

Training

It's about one in the morning and the whole house is dark and quiet. Alexander stays to the side of the house by the old maple tree. I scale the wall to Nathanial's room and sliding the window open, I climb inside without making a noise. Nathanial is sound asleep. I go over to the side of his bed and watch him for a few minutes. Alexander has open communication of thoughts with me; "*Can you see into Nathanial's dreams?*"

"*More clearly than I would like too.*"

Alexander's able to get into Nathanial's dream, and we both watch. I am quite surprised to see what's in there. Nathanial is dreaming about us, and our future. We seem so happy and everything seems perfect. I'm glad to see this is what he dreams about.

I can feel his dream just as if we are living it, so peaceful. Suddenly an awful looking vampire comes at us. Nathanial pushes me out of the way and begins to fight. It's time to wake him; I don't want this dream to continue.

I lean over and kiss him gently, "Nate, wake up! I came to check on you," I whisper softly.

He begins to stir and opens his eyes. "Sweetie, what are you doing here? Is everything okay?" he asks frantically, now wide awake and concerned.

"Ssh, we don't want to wake your family. Everything's fine. I just wanted to make sure you're okay with everything you learned today."

"I'm fine. You worry too much," he replies, still groggy.

"I know, I just can't help it. I don't want to lose you."

He sits up and holds me. "You never will! Nothing else matters to me anymore…you're everything to me. I admit I'm worried about you too. I don't want you to get hurt in this fight."

"I know; I promise we'll all be safe. I love you too, but I don't want you to give up everything for me. Everything you are and that you strive for is part of what I love about you. As for the fight, one of these nights when we're sparring and practicing, you can come and watch. I'll prove to you that I can kick some ass," I pledge.

"I know you can, and I'd love to come and watch," he agrees.

"Plus, don't forget we have Elijah on our side."

"What do you mean by that?"

"Well, Elijah is like 500 years old and was Embraced long before the world had a foothold on humanity; a time before technology was even a thought linking everyone together with the joys of Facebook. He was around when magic was used to heal and witches were the medicine men and women."

"That's pretty cool…I'd love to hear more one day, but how is any of that going to help protect you?"

"He's seen and fought in many wars and lived in the sixteenth century where they had to fight for everything they owned or wanted. Life was both simpler and more difficult back then. The king's men would just come and take what they wanted from your property. Nothing was ever guaranteed, and you could lose what you worked hard for in a moment while you slept. One night, Elijah lost his life and gained his eternity."

"He was Embraced for no reason?"

"A man wanted Elijah to work for him, but he refused. Later that night that man came to Elijah's homestead to Embrace him. He told Elijah that he owned him now and he must work for him. It took almost a century for Elijah to break free. He says the only good thing that came from his time as a prisoner for this man, is Florence. The man Embraced her to be his concubine after she refused him as well."

"Wow, they really have been through a lot!"

"We all have, but none more than Elijah and Florence. They'll protect us all, we are their family now."

"You sure do trust them, so I guess I should too." He takes my hand in his.

"Well, I just wanted to stop by and make sure you are okay after everything you have been learning… and here I go giving you even more. Now that I know you're okay I should go and let you sleep," I begin to get up.

"Not so fast!" He grabs a hold of my arm and pulls me back into him. "You can't just sneak into a guy's room, say hello and leave."

I let out a little chuckle. "Alex is waiting for me outside."

"Oh, well at least cuddle with me for a few minutes?" he asks.

"Sure." We cuddle up together on his bed, and he is asleep again in seconds.

I crawl back out the window and Alexander is waiting in the car for me.

"Do you feel better?"

"I do…at least a little bit," I answer.

We take the long way home, just looking around and making sure nothing is out of place. I really want to get this over with. I'm worried for the town's people; I find myself wanting to protect them all. In all my years I've never felt as welcome as I do here and now. In a little over a century, I've finally found a place to call home.

∞ ∞ ∞

Over the next few days, we begin working at Ms. Edwina's manor, helping the sisters prepare. I realize their fight will be strictly magical; they can't hold their own in a physical fight against vampires. I only hope that their powers and spells can withhold and destroy the Cerberus' powers. The sisters are said to be the most powerful of witches and can defeat anything, but as a friend, I still worry.

"Sophia, we'll be fine. Let us use our magic to help you. We'll be able to conjure up some good spells. The Cerberus won't know what hit them," Ebony tries to hearten me.

We begin spending our evenings in the field where I took Nathanial, sparring and physically preparing for the upcoming fight. Nathanial joins us tonight.

"So how exactly do you prepare for a vampire fight?" he inquires.

"We prepare just as any other physical training, including such things as cardio, upper body strength, lower body strength, speed, stealth, and agility. We always sprint up to the field and do about a hundred laps of the large open space; it really only takes a few minutes. Other warm-ups such as sit-ups, pushups, and lunges are all included. Once warmed up we take turns fighting…first up tonight will be Isaac and myself."

In a sarcastic tone, Nathanial says, "Great, so I get to watch my girlfriend get beat on, that sounds like a lot of fun."

"What makes you think he's going to be able to beat me?" I smirk.

We'll fight as if we are enemies and fighting for our survival, or at least the survival of those around us. We decide not to use our extra powers to start out with. We choose to fight with our physical strengths and speed, concentrating on our fighting skills. This makes things more even in our training because of the variety of our powers. I can heal others, so it won't help me in our fight. Isaac can control the elements; this can and will be a huge advantage when we fight the Cerberus. Against one another though, we just don't want to do any real damage to each other...more specifically me! We begin to fight; wrestling, hitting, and breaking bones and such. We all agree that it would not benefit any of us to take it easy on one another.

Our fight is going pretty good. *It's like UFC extreme*, I think to myself. Knowing that Isaac has the upper hand because he's been around longer, I put all my effort into the fight. With one swift move he lunges at me; I duck and am able to grab Isaac from behind. Flipping him over, I slam him into the ground. With an arch of his back, he jumps back to his feet, chasing after me. With lightning speed, I race up the side of a tree and flip to land behind him. Just as fast Isaac turns to face me, and with hand, to hand combat, we continue. My emotional ties to this area add passion to my fight. I don't want Nathanial, or his family hurt, killed or Embraced during all this chaos. From the corner of my eye, I see Nathanial, which encourages me to fight harder.

My entire family seems surprised at how well I'm holding my own against Isaac. The need to be aware of my surroundings draws my attention to Elijah. From what I can gather, it appears as though Elijah is telling Alexander to sneak into our fight, to try to distract us. He chooses to help Isaac in attacking me, I assume because they want to ensure my safety when I'm faced by multiples fighters. As Isaac and I are involved in our fight, throwing punches and kicks face to face, Alexander comes behind me. I sense him about to attack and move to the side with such stealth that he stumbles towards Isaac, throwing both of them off their fight. During our fight, we need to keep track of what is going on around us, to be aware of our surroundings and those involved. One moment of not paying attention can lose the whole fight.

I sense Nathanial freaking out, and I notice Elijah restraining him from interfering in the fight. This is even more of a distraction for me and could cost me the fight. I see him pushing and frantically trying to come to my aid. It's no problem for Elijah to restrain him, holding him simply with one arm over Nathanial's chest. With another glance over to Nathanial, that's what happens to me. Both Alexander and Isaac attack, and Alexander takes me down with a swift kick at my feet. Hitting the ground hard, I try to get my bearings, but before I can retreat, Isaac is above me with a tree branch ready for the kill. Isaac pounds the branch into the ground next to me and helps me to my feet.

"Good fight kid, you almost had me there," Isaac says as he brushes the dirt from himself.

With a smile, I respond, "Yeah, if Alex wouldn't have come in when he did I would have won that round."

"Oh, well, that's the price you pay for getting distracted, Sis," Alexander jokes and we walk towards the rest of the family.

"Sophia you did very well, but Nathanial seems to be a serious distraction for you," Elijah adds.

With disappointment, Nathanial lowers his head, "I'm so sorry Sophia. I couldn't stand to watch them hurting you."

"You have nothing to be sorry about Nate. I think it is best for you to try to distract Sophia. This will aid in her training," Elijah suggests.

Everyone agrees that it's best to distract me and teach me not to allow for distractions, while still remaining aware. I have to talk to him now that my fight is over; I can tell he is pretty upset with Isaac and Alexander.

"Are you going to be okay?" I ask.

"How can they gang up on you like this? I can't just stand here and watch two men beat on the woman I love. This is killing me! " Nathanial is furious, pacing back and forth wearing a path on the still brown grass.

"I love that you're concerned about me, but I'm fine, Nate. We need to do this; we have to be prepared. I know you want to help, but you must remember that I am stronger and faster… it's very difficult to hurt me. Fighting like this would kill you. You can help us, you just can't fight," I try to explain.

"I know all this, but that doesn't mean I enjoy sitting back and watching you get beat to the ground."

"I understand how hard this must be for you; just know I'm doing it to keep you, your family, and your friends safe."

"I do know that, and I'll help in any way I can. As Elijah suggested, I'll be here to distract you."

I can tell how hard this is for him and that hurts me, but we have to do it.

As the family gets back to sparring, I rest for a little while. Not only so I can have a break, but so Nathanial can also have a break. We just sit together on the edge of the clearing, watching the others fight. We continue training till early evening before returning home. We don't want to be out in case the Cerberus can sense us and arrive before we're ready for them. We don't know their powers, and one may have the ability to sense others with supernatural powers just as Caspian did.

"So, I'm able to spend the night again. I told my parents that all the boys are going snowboarding in the morning and I'm invited. I don't like to lie to my parents, but it does avoid questions," Nathanial says with a hint of remorse.

"You're so close to your family. I feel awful we can't let them know my family's secret, but it will just put them in danger," I confirm.

"I know, and that's why I do it."

∞ ∞ ∞

The family decides to take the rest of the night off from all things Cerberus. We've been wrapped up in planning and preparing since New Year's. School is starting again soon, and we need a night of relaxation.

"Mati and I are going to watch a movie in the family room; you two are welcome to join us," Alexander invites.

Elijah and Florence both head to the study to read a book, and Isaac and Constance both have to work the late shift at the hospital.

"So, do you want to watch a movie with Alex and Mati or just do our own thing?" I ask.

“Let’s just go chill by ourselves,” Nathanial suggests.

We head up to my room, crawl up on my bed and turn on some music. It’s so nice to just listen to the music and relax. We enjoy each other and start joking around a little.

“Sweetie, I was just wondering…”

“Yeah?”

“Exactly how ticklish are you?” Nathanial jumps on me and begins to tickle me.

I start squirming and laughing…I could easily push him off but it’s fun, it feels so normal. Lightly sitting on top of me, he instantly stops tickling me and slowly bends down to kiss me. I love feeling the weight of his body on top of me; it’s so comforting, like a big thick blanket on a cold winter night. The kiss sets fireworks off within my body again. His lips are as soft and gentle as a downy baby chick, moving in perfect synch with mine once again. Nathanial sits up and climbs off of me to kneel beside me, and I rise to my knees in front of him. Still kissing, we pause for a moment. He slowly runs his hands down my arms to my fingertips, intertwining his fingers with mine. Nathanial slowly lifts my arms above my head and then runs his hands back down my sides, without moving his eyes from mine. With a slow fluid motion, he lifts my shirt from my navel over my chest and slips it off. I yearn for him, needing him more than ever. As he’s slowly kissing me up and down my neck, I gently pull back and take his shirt off, tossing it to the floor next to mine. Running his hands down my bare back over my bra strap he whispers, “You are so beautiful. Your skin is so soft and creamy smooth. I’ve never imagined anything feeling so perfect,” he says as he slowly kisses my bare shoulder.

"I love you so much, Nate! You're so amazing." I run my hands over his perfectly chiseled chest. Leaning forward, kissing his chest, I slowly move my hands over his washboard abs.

Gently he pulls me into him so that we are skin to skin as he holds me. My hair's up in a ponytail, and Nathanial pulls the pony holder out, letting my hair fall to my shoulders. I melt as he runs his fingers through my tousled hair. The feel of his fingers running through my hair and down my back is electric. Being so close to the man of my dreams is indescribable.

I wonder if this is it. *Are Nathanial and I about to make love for the first time?* My heart begins to flutter with excitement and nervousness.

"Nate, have you ever done anything like this before? Have you ever had sex before?" I ask.

"No! I'd never really even kissed a girl, until you; unless you count Sara in my third-grade class," he laughs, "What about you?"

"There was a boy I dated for a while when I was sixteen…he was my first kiss. He was really just a friend, as I had no intimate feelings for him. Once my family promised my hand in marriage to the Duke we had to refrain from seeing each other. Then, before my wedding, I was Embraced and saved from being a baby-making factory for an old man. I guess now it's you stuck with an old woman." We both chuckle.

"I don't think of you like that; to me you're the woman I love, and that's the only thing that matters to me. You know the old cliché…'age doesn't matter'. I can understand that statement to its full extent now."

He grabs me in his arms and holds me close. We start falling on to the bed, entangled with one another. I've never felt so much passion before; I never even thought anything like this existed. How on earth did I ever become so lucky to have found Nathanial? I never want this feeling to end. Then I start thinking, *are we really ready for this? Am I ready for this? My family has all explained what it's like to have sex.* Alexander has explained the difference between human sex and vampire sex. He said it was exciting and exhilarating as a human, but as a vampire, it's like thousands of lightning bolts shooting through your body all at once. He says it's impossible to control our strength during intercourse. That during intercourse as a vampire every feeling and sensation is multiplied by millions. The part I find really interesting is the connection he described to me. There is a complete connection during intercourse, and one can feel every feeling and thought of the other. No secret can be kept because the one you're involved with will now know it all and know you like no other. There's no real way of explaining it. Alexander explained that I can seriously hurt Nathanial if we do have sex; that my thirst for his blood may drive me insane, and even be impossible to resist. Finally, he told me that's what happened with Caspian and Ashley. After 30 years I finally found out what drove my brother; Caspian, away from our family; the full details of the night we found Ashley covered in blood, and Caspian destroyed over what he had done. It just seems like so much to handle, and I can't help but question if we're really ready for such a step.

I want to share this with Nathanial, but I never want to hurt him. I'm strong emotionally now when it comes to my relationship with Nathanial…maybe we can do this, and I might be able to control myself. Then I start becoming abundantly aware of his scent, his blood coursing through his veins, and his increased heart rate. I begin to question what's happening and if this is a bad idea…I don't think I can fully trust myself. I've been told that since his blood has been planted within me from the day of his attack, I should be able to resist him, but I just don't think I'm willing to risk it. I'm not ready for Nathanial to meet the same fate that Ashley did so many years earlier.

"Nate, I don't know if this is a good idea. I'm scared I might hurt you, or worse," I confess.

"Sophia, I know you'd never harm me. I trust you completely, but if you aren't ready for this we can wait. I love you and I want the day we make love to be special, and memorable. I don't want you to be scared or resent it. So never mind, we should wait until we are both ready and the time is right," he comforts me.

We share so much passion for each other it's hard to resist, but we have to for his safety. Maybe one day I'll have more confidence in myself, but today is not the day.

I decide to change into my pajamas, so we can just fall asleep in each other's arms. It's the perfect way to end the night. I don't sleep for long, but I enjoy cuddling up to him. He smells so good and I love watching him sleep, so peaceful and warm. When I'm in his arms I finally feel like I belong. Then my mind drifts to Danika. She's been fairly absent again lately, and with the family so wrapped up in training, no one has really noticed. I can't help but think she's up to no good. She can't be anywhere near the fight, she's far too young. I'd like to know what she's up to; to have somebody watching her.

∞ ∞ ∞

Morning comes, and this means our last day of winter break. Ms. Edwina and her granddaughters arrive at our place early. We want to organize all of the potions and spells we'll need in the fight against the Cerberus. This way the supplies are ready when we need them since we'll be at school most of the day. The arrangements with Nate's parents have been set. They believe that Elijah and Florence have already left town and Isaac and Constance will be taking the rest of us in a few days, with the exception of Danika of course, she'll stay with them.

"The Renata contacted me early this morning. The Cerberus are getting closer; we have to be ready. I think it may be time to store the potions and spells up at the clearing, rather than here at the house," Elijah explains. "That way no matter where we are when this goes down, we have everything we need already at the clearing. We want to direct them away from town. This will be the best way to protect the people."

"We can use that safe in my room. I already made some camouflage for it. I can hide it well, so that if someone does stumble near it, they will never realize it," Alexander confirms.

"I have to ask, what is so special and magical about the clearing? It's got to be more than the spells…I mean what will draw them there rather than into town? How can we know they will sense it?" Danika releases her concerns.

Isaac smiles and says, "We suspect that one of the leaders can sense powers and magical or supernatural energies, so if we all congregate there it should draw them to us."

"Also, my dear, the clearing was once used as a magical ritual ground, and many of the area witches have chosen the area to cross from the mortal life into Summerland," Ms. Edwina explains.

Danika looks even more perplexed now, "What's Summerland?"

Ebony sits next to Danika as Ms. Edwina continues, "Summerland is where we witches go upon our demise, our death until we are chosen to return to the Mother Earth."

Potions and spells should be organized into different categories such as power disabling, protection, healing, freezing, binding, and enhancement. Matilda suggests we color code the vials as an extra safety measure. We have to ensure all enhancement potions are kept in different vials as to not throw them at the Cerberus…we don't want to enhance their strength or powers. Ms. Edwina will control these during the fight. The girls also made her a protection broach; she can't fight at her age, and we need her protected just as Matt and Nathanial are by their watch and wristband. As she's very old and we fear for her, she'll be put in a type of invisible bubble for protection. The rest of us can't use such protection because it does affect our powers as we suspected and we're unclear as to how it'll affect us while fighting.

The girls made protection potions so that if one of us gets injured and needs time to heal, they can hit us with one and the Cerberus won't be able to get to us. This might help, but unless I am near the injured when the protection spell was thrown, I won't be able to get to them either. That's why they also made healing potions to enhance the increased speed of healing. I feel confident that all our bases are covered. As vampires, we can heal and regenerate, but the length of time depends on the severity of the injuries. My ability allows me to speed the healing process to only moments.

Nathanial's pleased. "Thank you for involving me so much in the planning, but I'm still not happy about having to stay home when you're risking everything."

I feel bad because he has no one to talk to about all this. Matt has no clue about the supernatural and anyone else that does know has supernatural abilities. I can only imagine that it'd be nice for Nathanial to have someone to talk to and confide in.

"I've been thinking of confiding in Matt. He means so much to me and was there for me when I first found out I was a witch. Everything that happened at school, with my powers, well he didn't even react to it. He's been nothing but patient and supportive. I just don't want him to think I'm a freak," Ebony says nervously.

"Wow, that was good timing," I chuckle.

"What was?"

"I was just thinking about Matt not knowing and how it would be nice for Nathanial to have a friend to confide in."

"I guess great minds do think alike," she laughs.

I encourage her, knowing how hard it is to have a secret like this. I have a really good feeling about Matt; there's just something special about him, and Matilda sees his and Ebony's two souls together. Alexander still can't read him and although he finds it frustrating, he believes it's for a reason. We all know he's good because of his soul. When we first met Matt, Matilda said he has a white soul, something she's only seen once before.

"Ebony, if you want help talking to Matt we can be there for you. It may be good for him to know that Nate is so understanding and accepting of everything, and yet still a mortal," I volunteer.

"That just may be the way to do this," she agrees with relief. "I have plans with him...in about an hour. Why don't you and Nate come with me? No better time than now. I think he should know before the battle; I should probably get this over with before I lose all my nerve."

"Great. I can finally talk to a buddy about this," Nathanial interjects.

"What am I? Just some scary old vampire, I guess," Alexander jokes.

Nathanial smirks. "Yeah, you're absolutely terrifying."

We all know he just wants someone to talk to that's in the same situation as him or at least a similar situation. Being in love with a supernatural being must be difficult. This way Matt and Nathanial can rely on one another for support when things are out of their control. I also feel that it adds safety to the situation for Nathanial because now there will be two mortals that know about us. It protects him in a sense; with Matt knowing what is going on, they can keep one another from interfering.

Chapter 6

Confiding

Ebony, Nathanial, and I walk into her family's manor and try to get comfortable. We need to prepare to let another mortal into our secret world. I can only hope that for Ebony's sake Matt can handle this information.

"Matt will be here shortly. I don't even know where to start," Ebony starts to freak out about spilling her secret to Matt.

She loves him and is scared to lose him, while on the other end, Nathanial is excited because he really doesn't know much about witches. He's asked me in the past to explain more of the history, but now he'll have more of his questions answered first hand, from the witch's mouth.

Matt's right on time…he's always very punctual. Nathanial gets up and greets him at the door. Ebony and I just remain in the family room, while I continue to try to get her to relax. We can hear the boys bantering; I can hear every word, breathe and move as if I was right next to them.

"Hey there bro, nice to see you," Matt says. I hear their hands slap together and whoosh through the air as he shakes hands with Nathanial.

I've learned to control my hearing, but when I allow myself to listen I can hear the slightest movement. I can hear both the sound of their hands clapping as they grip and a swooshing sound as they move their clasped hands through the air. To anyone else they might just hear a light clap, but to me, it sounds like thunder clapping and a tidal wave approaching land. My hearing can come in handy at times, but without the ability to control it, one could go insane.

"Hey, how you doing?" Nathanial asks.

"Good, Good! Are you and Sophia hanging out with us today?"

"Yeah, that's the plan. We figure we could all just hang here and chat. We have the place to ourselves." Nathanial is beginning to prep Matt for our discussion.

The boys come to join us in the family room, and Matt opens his arms to Ebony. They embrace each other as if it's been a year since they last saw one another. I can tell Ebony's holding him like she thinks it will be the last time he'll hold her in his arms.

"What's wrong Eb? You seem a little down," Matt observes.

"We just need to talk," she sighs. "I have something to tell you, and I'm not sure how you'll handle it."

"Are you breaking up with me?" he asks with concern, reaching out to hold her hand.

"NO!" she exclaims. "You know how I feel about you. I need to talk to you about my family and our history,"

"Okay, well go on. There is nothing that you can say or do to change your family history, I care for you now, your family can't affect how I feel. Whatever you have to tell me about your family isn't going to alter who you are, so I don't see how anything will change between us."

"But that's just it; this changes everything about me, about who I am," she tilts her head up slightly to look in his eyes. "Okay, well let's all sit down. Sophia knows everything, but we want Nate to hear the details too. He knows the basics already. It all involves Sophia as well," Ebony begins to explain.

"I thought you two just met?" Matt asks.

"We did. But our families have a history," she confirms.

"Are you two related?"

"No. But I'll explain everything" she insists.

Listening to everything happening, I walk into the kitchen to get drinks for everyone and then take my seat next to Nathanial after ensuring everyone has a beverage. "Okay, now that everyone's here I'll begin, Sophia please jump in at any time," Ebony suggests, almost pleading with a shaky voice.

"Only if you need me too…this is your story," I reply.

"I really don't know where to begin," Ebony admits as she nervously twirls her hair between her fingers.

"Just start at the beginning and don't be so nervous," Matt encourages.

Ebony switches from twirling her hair to fiddling with the necklace she is wearing as she sits at the head of the family room across from Matt. I don't ever remember seeing anyone this nervous before, and then I remember when I told Nathanial about my secret, and realize I know exactly how she feels. Her insides are twisting and turn, she feels like vomiting, her heart's racing and it's hard to catch her breath. She feels like her world is about to come crashing down and end. That's how I felt, and nothing can stop it.

"Well, I guess a brief history on my family is in order. My family originated in Salem many years ago. My ancestors were witches here in the 1600's. In the early 1900's my great-grandmother was one of the most powerful witches around, along with my Grams who was just a young girl at the time. The two of them would help the immortals in need; ones that had kind souls and meant no harm to the mortals. These immortals are called vampires." She pauses to gauge Matt's reaction.

He's extremely calm and only trying to see Nathanial's and my reaction, to his surprise we are equally as calm and just watching him.

Ebony continues, "When my sister and I were born it was a magical event within the community; two witches from a strong family heritage of powerful witches. When I turned sixteen, I began to notice changes within myself. I'd think of something and it would slowly move toward me. I realized I'm telekinetic; I can move things with my mind. My sister has powers too. Now that we are both of age within the witch community, we're considered The Magnificent Ones, the most powerful of all witches in the world. That's what happened that day at school with Mel when the two of us were arguing by the lockers and everything flew open." She stops again to see how Matt's handling the new information. "You seem so calm, is everything okay?" she questions.

"Honestly, I'm just trying not to laugh," he replies.

"What? This is no joke!"

"No…no, that's not what I mean. I'm all too familiar with the supernatural. I believe you…I've even heard of you and your sister. I just never knew it was you," he explains. "I guess I should have figured it out that day at school with Mel. I realized then you had powers, I just never put the pieces together. I mean, I assumed you were a witch, but you being one of The Magnificent Ones never crossed my mind."

"Really? What do you mean by familiar?" Ebony asks.

"Well, let's just say I have a family history too," Matt smiles.

"Okay…I guess I'll explain a little more and then you can explain to me?" Ebony suggests. The relief in Ebony is visible, she calms right down, her heart rate returns to normal and she lets out a sigh, getting control of her breathing again.

"Sounds good to me," Matt agrees.

"I really only found out about this around the same time as my incident with Mel; before that, I thought it was nothing more than stories. Since then I've been working to improve my skills and powers. I've been learning spells and how to make potions. My sister and I are getting pretty good at it too," she boasts with a hint of pride.

"Now you say you are familiar with the supernatural, but is it just witches or do you know about other supernatural forces as well?" Ebony wonders.

He replies with a smirk on his face, "Well let's just say that not too much would surprise me."

"Okay, well do you believe in vampires? Because I happen to know for a fact, that they do exist."

"I'm aware of them, but don't have much extra information on them. What I know isn't much more than what you can get off the Internet," he admits.

"Okay, well then I guess I can continue," Ebony says.

"Now some of the other things that have been happening in Wenham are that vampires have returned; the ones that are here are kind, good spirited and feed only on animals or donated blood. The bad news is that the evil vampires are heading this way; they believe that our area is rich in powers, and they're right. This is creating an inevitable supernatural war. The evil vampires that are called the 'Cerberus' should arrive here in days, and the leaders of the civilized vampires, the 'Renata', are tracking them here," she tries to explain.

"How is it you know so much about vampires? Is it because of your family history?" Matt inquires.

"Sort of, the reason I know so much is because I know the vampires that live here," she confesses.

"Who? Do I know them?" he asks.

"May I interrupt?" I request.

"Please do," Ebony insists, with a sense of relief.

"It's not safe for mortals to know about vampires. Only a few know they really exist and those are only the most trustworthy people. With that said, the vampires she's referring to are my family. All eight of us are vampires. We haven't harmed humans in over 80 years. It's been difficult at times, but we all help one another to stay true to our beliefs," I confess as Nathanial holds my hand supportively.

"Okay…and Nate, you know all this?" Matt asks, surprised by this revelation.

"I do, I know everything. Sophia saved my life the day of the attack in the park. If it was not for her healing me, I'd be dead. Her family's like heroes to me," Nathanial declares.

"I understand your family's very amazing. I assume you'll all be involved in this war with the Cerberus?" Matt seems to be sucking up; I can sense his heart rate increasing with the new revelation.

"First off, Matt I don't want you to worry; we're still the same people you have hung out with for months, just with a little history. Even if you can't accept this, you are safe. We only ask that you keep this a secret. Secondly, my family will be the main players in the war. With Ebony and her family, we should be successful," I explain.

"Not a problem; I think we all have secrets in this room that will need to be kept. Maybe it's time for me to share mine. Maybe then you will realize you have nothing to worry about, Ebony." Matt goes to sit next to her and holds her hand.

"Sure, but I bet it's not as surprising as mine or Sophia's news," Ebony laughs.

"I'll take that bet," he chuckles. "Well, just as your families have history, mine does as well. The thing is, Ebony, it ties in with yours. Have you learned about 'guardians' yet?" Matt asks.

"Yeah, a little bit. A guardian is kind of angel that helps and leads witches to protect mortals from evil," Ebony shares.

"Yeah kinda, they actually help any supernatural but historically it's been, witches. But did you know that they're chosen even before death, actually from the day they are born if not before? Guardians are trained and prepared for their afterlife. It is similar to witches; you are born to it and it is passed down through the generations."

"No, that I didn't know." Ebony seems surprised that Matt knows so much about guardians; she sits and listens intently with her deep brown eyes wide on Matt.

"The reason I know this is because my great-grandfather was a guardian, and he has now joined The Great Ones. I'm also chosen to be one. I've been training from a young age, learning the history of witches, guardians and all, or at least most, things supernatural. I'll have powers once I join the others in the afterlife. I'll be able to heal just like I assume Sophia can, and I've been learning about how to transport myself through time and space, called astral crossing or projection…it's pretty cool. Anything I do once I become a guardian; everything I do must be for the greater good of man, or I'll be stripped of all powers and memories related to being a guardian," he explains.

This is cool, now we have even more help and complete honesty within our circle. The excitement inside me builds, accepting that we were meant to be here.

"Okay, let me get this straight. I'm the only one with no special story, no powers...," Nathanial begins to rant.

"Nate, have you ever noticed how most people confide in you, how people can't keep things from you?" Matt questions.

Ebony and I share a glance and chuckle at the comment.

"I guess so…that's just 'cause I am too nice to tell them I'm not interested," Nathanial pouts.

"Naw man, that's your gift, you just didn't know it. You have the gift to expel information out of ones who are hiding things. You're like a truth serum. You might not have supernatural powers, but you're a good guy. We all just have to find what is special about us. You make people feel comfortable and they trust you without you even trying. Someone else might be extremely helpful or kind to strangers. Everyone is special in their own way; some good and some bad. I don't have 'powers'…at least not until I am dead. And then who knows what powers I may have," Matt confirms.

"Nate, I have to agree with Matt. When we first met I had such a hard time keeping everything from you. My entire family felt it; we talked about it, and none of us understood what was happening. We were drawn to you and felt instant comfort; we felt the need to learn more about you and to tell you more than we should. I was so relieved when you confronted me about my past. It meant I didn't have to fight what I wanted to tell you," I admit for the first time. "And Matt, I disagree that you don't have a gift yet. You can relax and calm people."

"Yeah, that is standard for future guardians. We need to have that effect on people to get them to listen to us, even if the guardian doesn't know what they are yet."

I'm feeling so relieved with all the confessions going on. The fact that my family isn't the only ones affected by Nathanial's kind of truth ability is interesting too. I'm glad to finally understand why now and believe that we can all learn so much from Matt. We sit and listen as he explains his training in greater detail. He's done extensive research on the supernatural and we'll all gain from his knowledge.

We all chuckle. It is remarkable that Matt knows so much about witches and their history; I think Ebony's relieved. Nathanial understands a little more now, and the four of us begin discussing the threats heading our way. Matt's giving us some good insight on other threats we may face down the road. I think we're not only forming great friendships but great allies in the fight against all Cerberus and whatever else may come our way.

Matt starts explaining more about the guardians to us, "When a chosen one passes on, their spirit joins The Great Ones in a magical realm and they begin to complete their training. This training consists of all the things they can't learn while still alive, including all the powers they gain and extensive practice. Once The Great Ones have completed the formal training, the guardian can return to Earth. When they return they can live as a magical human figure. To everyone that sees them they appear to be human; even supernaturals can't tell until the guardian reveals themselves to the being they're assigned to work with."

"What kinds of things can't you learn until after you die?" Nathanial inquires.

"Well, like I mentioned earlier, various kinds of astral travel can't be learned until you are in spirit form. As a mortal, our spirit can travel to various realms through meditation, but the physical body doesn't actually leave, the only exception is magic. A guardian can travel through various realms and even physical places. Guardians can…well, be here one minute and physically appear in another place a moment later. Leaving no trace of the guardian in the first place. It's kinda hard to explain…is this making any sense?"

"Yeah, so instead of driving to my house from yours, as a guardian you just magically appear," Nathanial confirms.

Matt continues, "A guardian doesn't age, and shouldn't become involved with a mortal. A relationship can affect their assignment, although history has proven that some guardians do have relationships with mortals and are still successful with their assignments. Others have failed miserably, and people have died and suffered because of it. They can also be assigned to many different witches, and when one of the beings they are assigned to calls for them or is in danger, the guardian hears the call. As I mentioned before a guardian can work with any supernatural being that works for the greater good, it's most commonly witches. The Great Ones help lead guardian's and have many rules, in order to protect their identity and that of the guardians and supernatural they help."

This is extremely interesting, to hear stories of a supernatural power or entity that we know nothing about. I always enjoy learning more about the world we live in. It's also nice to learn that there's others fighting to protect mankind. Maybe the universe isn't as evil as I have begun to believe, and maybe we are here for a reason. Our little group of friends is so diverse and connected in some supernatural way; this can't just be a coincidence.

Although Matt's unable to help us in our fight he could report to his trainers about the situation. Maybe they'll be able to offer us help, a type of protection or warning. We need to find out who Ebony and Eliza's guardian is. Matt then explains that they try to remain undercover until a time when they're needed, or their being is needed to help with something important. Well, now is that time, even if their guardian isn't aware of it yet. I just hope that we can find him or her soon. Although Matt explained guardians help all kinds of supernatural beings, he also explained, for the most part, its witches.

"Now that I explained about my history and future for that matter, and since I'm fully aware of witches, I would like to learn more about vampires," Matt requests.

"What would you like to know?" I ask.

"Well you say you haven't harmed humans in over 80 years; so how is it that you survive? Don't you need blood?"

"Yes, we do, but my family and I survive off a combination of donated blood and animal blood. It doesn't taste as good, and we need to feed more frequently as it doesn't keep us as strong. We're very committed to living peacefully among mortals. So, this is the way we manage to keep the peace. Florence is very good at creating various foods and meals from the blood we use; we all have our favorites just as a normal family."

"Are there others like you?

"Yes a several, but most, although living peacefully, still feed on humans, without killing them. The mortal is then compelled or hypnotized to forget what happened. Florence actually has a gift to take that process a step further and implant new memories."

"So how is it that you can go out in the sun? I know from my training that burning and some other stuff is true about vampires."

"Yes, normally that's correct to a point, but thanks to Ebony's family and a magical bloodstone we call our day crystal, we can now live more like mortals. When Ms. Edwina was a child she helped her mother create a talisman for each of us. There are a few others that have been helped by witches as well. Also, those that are centuries old can go out as long as they don't go directly into the sun and remain in the shadows. However, in general, vampires will burn if exposed to the sun."

"Okay, I think I am beginning to understand," Matt smiles. "Can you tell me more about these evil vampires heading this way; what kind of danger can we expect?"

"We really aren't sure, but it won't be good. They've already killed in the New York area and have begun their descent to the New England area. We believe they have plans to overtake the governing body, the Renata. This governing body is also made up of long-lost ancestors of the Cerberus clan.

"Okay, so what do we do? How can I help?"

Ebony and I both look at one another; I don't even need Alexander here to sense her emotions and know exactly what she is thinking. Neither of us wants the ones we love to face any harm.

"You can't do anything; you don't have any powers that can help in the fight against them. Nate and you should stay together and protect each other. My family will handle this with the help of Ebony's family." Raw emotion coming through in my plea, I beg them both to be safe and far away from this fight.

"I'll talk to my trainers and try to see if The Great Ones have any information regarding the Cerberus."

“That’ll be great, thank you, Matt.” I can tell Nathanial has a new-found sense of relief as he rests back in his seat, pulling his right ankle over his left knee.

“Dude you don’t know how glad I am that I won’t be stuck alone in this crazy secret anymore,” Nathanial says with enthusiasm. “Even if you’re not exactly mortal like me.”

We chuckle, and Matt adds, “I am until I die…and who is mortal once they die anyway?”

I continue to explain a little vampire history to Matt in condensed form; he’ll learn more as time goes by, plus Nathanial can fill in the blanks. Nathanial will soon be a vampire pro; he’s borrowed Elijah’s journals that he keeps as a sort of history book for reference. Finally finishing off with the serious stuff, we can relax a little before going home for the night. School will be interesting tomorrow with all the new faces we’ve met. I still can’t believe what a huge success our New Year’s party was, although I still wonder where Danika took off to that night and if anything happened.

Here and now though, I’m really beginning to feel such comfort. I finally feel like I belong; our close friends all have some special secret. I believe there’s some reason bigger than any of us could imagine that brought us here. For now, we’ll just need to handle the Cerberus problem, and then maybe we can figure out why we’ve all come together.

Matt looks at Ebony, holds her hand, looks deeply into her eyes and asks, “Are you feeling a little better, more comfortable now that you know we all have secrets?”

“I do…I feel a great sense of relief, and to know that you and your family are involved with the supernatural is comforting.” She lets a small smile slip out.

“We really should head home; it’s getting late,” I suggest.

“Sophia’s right; vacation is over and back to jail…ah, I mean school…we go. We’ll catch up with you at school,” Nathanial rises, stretching out his hand to shake Matt’s.

“Yeah, of course. See you bright and early,” Matt shakes his hand and they do their silly little half man hug, patting one another on the shoulder.

I begin taking the trays of drinks back to the kitchen for Ebony and gently place the glasses in the sink, wipe the tray down and put it away. I say my goodbyes, and whisper to Ebony, “Call me in a bit.”

She nods in agreement.

Chapter 7

Protecting

School starts back in with a bang, Alexander and Matilda drop me off at Nathanial's house and we drive to school in his new car. It seems like the entire student body stops and stares as we pull up. The car my 'parents' gave Nathanial was pretty nice, and it was a known fact his family could not have bought him the car. No one saw it at the New Year's party, because Nathanial was there first.

"Dude! Win the lottery over Christmas? Nice car!" Ben, Nathanial's friend from football, begins scoping the car. He's always ready to tease us, or at least tease Nathanial, but it's all in good fun.

"It was a Christmas gift," Nathanial smiles at me.

"I guess someone was good this year," Ben pokes.

Without divulging that it was a gift from my family he just replies, "Yeah, Santa was good to me this year." Then we head to class.

It's a pretty typical day with the exception of everyone greeting us now. The seven of us, which includes Danika, eat lunch together again, just like before winter break. We quietly discuss what is going on around us and laugh about everyone's chatter about us. I would have thought that after our New Year's party the chatter would die down a little, but I think it may be worse now, albeit nicer. After lunch we finish out our classes and head home, just continuing through the motions of being regular teens. Nathanial, Ebony, and Matt all come to our house to study, bags and books in tote; midterms are later this month, and everyone wants to be well prepared.

We start working on our homework and then we can study for our midterm exams. As the others study, my family and I excuse ourselves to go on a scouting trip to ensure we remain well fed. We've been so caught up in training we haven't stocked up on animal blood. We're trying to ensure fresh human donation every other day, but don't want to overdo it. We've worked very hard to sustain our life without causing harm to others, and too much fresh blood could result in bloodlust. Danika's remained on her usual diet of blood from the blood bank combined with animal blood; she wouldn't be able to handle fresh blood, and definitely not straight from a mortal.

"Danika, you can stay here with our guests; I have your dinner prepared in the kitchen, as well as some snacks for our guests," Florence informs.

∞ ∞ ∞

"Can you believe we caught a moose, a bear, and some smaller animals?" Alexander says with excitement. This will help to replenish our stock nicely; the larger animals allow for us to extract more. We're able to get several bags of blood from one large animal.

We all enjoy the thrill of the hunt; after all, it is our nature. This's not something we normally all go out together and do; because of our diet we just remove the necessary amount of blood and store it. However, because we don't know what's to come, we make sure we have extra to store.

"I'm amazed that we saw a pair of wolves. I thought they've been extinct in the area for over a hundred and fifty years when they were run out by hunters," I admit.

"There's been a few reports of sightings over the last few years, but never confirmed," Elijah announces. "I think it is best to avoid them. We don't want to cause the extinction of an animal in the area and interrupt the natural order of things. If there are only a few left in the area, we're best to leave them be."

Isaac agrees, "Did you notice the unusual way there are several other animals hovering around the two wolves? Wolves don't usually keep company with other breeds of animals; this is very suspicious."

We brush it off for the time being and hurry back home. While the others are still studying, I run upstairs to shower; I don't want Nathanial to smell the carnage on me. Although he knows what just happened and accepts it, I'm still concerned how he'll react. It doesn't take me long to get all cleaned up, and I head back down to the library, where they're discussing our wolf sighting. "I couldn't hear the thoughts of the wolves clearly, but I did get feelings from them as well, as the other animals that were nearby. I've never experienced such feelings before, at least not from an animal. They're usually a blank slate for me. I just don't understand this," Alexander admits.

Constance adds, "When I tried to see something around them, I kept seeing a group of men. I've never had a vision like that before."

We all got a different feeling around these wolves, and agree they aren't right for hunting. Something is amiss here and we need to figure it out before it's too late.

Nathanial starts to explain a story to us. “Here’s a little history lesson for you. The Agawam tribe owned the land that’s now Wenham many years ago, and they swore to always protect it from evil. It’s said that some of the tribesmen would shapeshift into wolves, cougars, hawks and such to scout the land and ensure its safety. It’s believed that these men become shapeshifters after they have gone on a spirit walk and had an animal walk with them. It is like a calling from their ancestors. There are light rumors that they still patrol the area today.”

“That makes a lot of sense as to why I had feelings from them because they’re people,” Alexander speculates.

“I don’t really know if this is true, or just a myth…I just don’t know what to believe or not to believe anymore. In the past few months I’ve come to learn that there is truth behind myths,” Nathanial admits.

“I think it is worth looking into,” Matt encourages.

We agree that Matt and Nathanial will go out to the local reserve and check into things. We don’t want them to think we are a threat, and we don’t want to accidentally kill one of them. They could be nice to have around when the Cerberus arrive; wolves and cougars have very sharp teeth good to rip apart the limbs of our enemies. Any other animal will also be of use as they all have something that could assist us in our fight.

I’ll tell Elijah everything we learn later this evening when I speak to him. Alexander and I begin to help Nathanial, Matt, and Ebony study for the exams. I’m pretty sure that we all will do just fine. Florence brings in some refreshment for our friends and we soon call it a night. Tomorrow will be a busy day. I’m very nervous about the boys going to find the Agawam ancestors; I hope they’ll be safe from harm. I think maybe one of us should follow them without their knowledge, just to be safe. Alexander is tapped into my thoughts again and agrees. We'll discuss it with our family shortly. Then I can do some research on the tribe.

∞ ∞ ∞

The following day at school we discuss what Matt and Nathanial will say to the Agawam tribe if they find them. We all agree that it'll be alright for the boys to admit to our secret. Never in my existence have we admitted to others our true identity, we've followed the six traditions. Now it seems like we are an open book. If anything, we want to confirm the presence of shapeshifters. Of course, we don't want to harm them, or the wolves – it's important to keep the life cycle going, but it's too bad the actual wolves are near extinction in the area…they can make for a decent meal. Later in the day Matt and Nathanial will head out to the reserve. It's only a thirty-five minute drive to Andover where the tribe settled after the sale of Wenham. We're not completely sure if any tribe members are Agawam descendants since European disease wiped out most of the tribe in 1617. From what I'm learning in my research the numbers were decreased to 3000 from over 30,000, and the remaining members disbanded and joined various surrounding tribes. I continue to research them throughout the day, passing information to the boys.

The two young men are fully prepared to meet the tribe. They decide to call ahead and ask for a tour of the reservation, stating it is research for a school paper; this will be their way in. They have the research on the Agawam Indians that I've done and are prepared with many questions. If any ancestors still survive and are at this reservation, our boys will find out. Elijah and Alexander remain nearby, and mentally connected, while the boys are on their quest. It seems like they've been gone for hours, but in reality, it has only been 90 minutes and it is over an hour's drive round trip. It's time for me to try and relax a little again.

∞ ∞ ∞

When the boys finally return, Matt starts explaining how they met a young man about eighteen years old, named Dakota Williams. "He knew of the myth or legend as the tribe called it but seemed to be hiding something more. He introduced us to his father Tamo. Tamo explained to Nathanial and I that the Agawam Indians return to the homeland to monitor things, and more so when danger is nearing. Since the native or original Agawam's are all deceased, it's now the responsibility of the few descendants left to protect what once was theirs. They told us they shapeshift and protect the land. The father and son seem very open to sharing the history of the Agawam tribe as if they already knew we were there to help."

Matt and Nathanial both appear elated to be doing their part in the war. Nathanial continues with the story, "They showed us ancient artifacts from the time their ancestors spent in the Wenham area. Tamo and Dakota appear to be very proud men and are very happy that their history isn't being forgotten."

After some time, the boys explain that they felt like it was time to open up a little. Tamo told Matt that he and his son have been experiencing weird happenings recently. Nathanial also explained about his attack at the winter formal, but he proceeded cautiously.

"They agree with us that something's been changing in the New England area. Because the native community is so spiritual, they sense it too," Matt mentions. "I told them that I've been feeling a strong presence in Wenham, and don't feel good about it."

"Tamo began to question me and Matt on our beliefs of the supernatural, and as we spoke we tried to gauge Mr. William's reaction. We both admitted that we believe in a lot more than most of the townsfolk. We explained that most of the people believe that some women hundreds of years ago believed they were witches and were persecuted, but today's people don't actually believe that's true, or that witches are real. Matt said that the two of us believe anything is possible. The Williams agreed," Nathanial explains. He continues by telling us, "After Matt and I explained a little of what is happening in Wenham and about the approaching threat, Tamo voiced his concern about vampires and what could happen in the area. We opened up even more and assured Tamo that we have friends of supernatural decent that want to solve this matter quickly and quietly."

"Along with Nathanial's ability to get people to open up to him and our honesty, Tamo finally felt at peace" Matt adds, "The level of comfort others feel around me, and Nate may have helped them to open up."

"Tamo confided in us that his family are the descendants of Agawam Indians and that the legend is true. The past few months more and more of the descendants began to change; he also mentioned that it happens around the age of 16. He explained to us that they sense a great danger approaching and they've seen vampires feeding in the region. Nathanial explained about your family and that you lived peacefully. He told Tamo your family doesn't want to harm them during your scouting trips," Matt explains to us.

"I also explained about The Magnificent Ones, and how the witches and vampires are working together to protect the region from harm and evil; telling them how your families make a very good team and have worked well together for many years. This time will be no different, and we hope the descendants will join us in the fight," Nathanial adds with enthusiasm. The smile on his face proves he is proud of their accomplishment

Matt adds, "Tamo asked if we also sensed danger. We explained in detail about the Cerberus fight that is coming. Tamo and Dakota asked what they can do to help. We invited them to join us at fight practice tonight in the clearing. The Williams agreed and said they would bring more as well. I hope that's alright with you?"

Alexander smiles, "Of course, that's why we sent you."

This is great news; now we'll have more help to win the battle against the Cerberus, assuming it's is not a trap and that the descendants of the Agawam Indians can be trusted. We need to be cautious tonight; it isn't customary for vampires and other supernatural beings to associate, with the exception of witches, but tonight we'll receive them in a warm manner.

It's almost six o'clock; Florence makes sure that all the mortals are well fed. She made veal and pasta for dinner. Nathanial, Matt, and Ebony are all enjoying their dinner. Ebony's sister is meeting us at the clearing at quarter past six tonight and the Williams were told half past. We don't want to stay out too late. Before we know it, it's time to leave. Nathanial drives up with Matt and Ebony. The rest of us head up on foot since it's faster; we arrive there before all the others, so we start some dodging exercises and warm up. Once the others arrive we prepare Eliza for our new allies that will be joining us soon. Alexander senses the newcomers nearing; they seem to be running a perimeter, to ensure this we aren't trying to trap them. Once comfortable they begin to join us in the clearing. We greet them one at a time; two wolves, two cougars, a hawk, and a mountain lion. We introduce ourselves, and suddenly they all disappear into the forest. In shock we begin looking around; we can hear the rustling of the bushes that resembles the sound of crumpling paper as the frozen ground cracks beneath their feet. In an instant, six men walk out of the forest and cautiously approach to greet us.

"Sorry for leaving so abruptly; we wanted to be in human form to discuss matters with you. My name is Tamo; I'm the leader of the pack per se, and this is my son Dakota."

"We're pleased to make your acquaintance. Nate and Matt told us all about you; we're glad you decided to join us," Elijah offers his hand out to Tamo.

"You as well. The others here are Makya, Shilah, Mika, and Skah," he introduces as each young man steps forward. "We are descendants of the Agawam tribe and sworn to protect the land from enemies. We were told you are expecting some rogue vampires to arrive soon?" Tamo inquires.

Elijah explains to the group what we know, and how we are preparing. The pack agrees to assist us in every way they can. We continue by showing them some of our sparring moves and they take turns jumping in. They're very good, very strong; the weakened Cerberus will have their work cut out for them. Ebony and Eliza demonstrate some of their spells and potions to the animal pack. They appear very impressed.

It is now nine o'clock. We agree to meet again tomorrow and every night until the Cerberus arrives. Constance and Alexander confirm it won't be long now. They're both sensing the danger. We extend an invitation for the Williams and their pack to join us at our house. We feel it will be good to get to know one another, before entrusting our safety to them and vice versa.

Chapter 8

Changes

Nathanial drives me home since it's on his way, and when we arrive at the house, he leans in and gives me a goodnight kiss. He walks around the car to let me out and walks me up to the door. "Sweetie, I'm wondering if you mind coming by my house tonight after everyone's settled for the night? I want to hold you close tonight, I'm worried about you and the fight. Plus, it's a great excuse to get you alone in my room," he chuckles.

"Yeah. I can do that," I agree to sneak in some time after midnight.

Entering the house, I see the family's all there discussing something; it looks serious. I notice our new shapeshifting friends from the Agawam descendants decided to join us too. When I take a better look I notice Cato, our contact from the Renata. I hope that Cato isn't aware of Nathanial and me outside a moment ago. I glance at Alexander and he confirms we're in the clear. With the presence of all the other supernatural beings, I'm glad Nathanial didn't come in to say goodnight.

"Cato, it's nice to see you again, I wish it were under better circumstances," I greet him.

"As do I, Sophia," Cato replies.

"I assume there's news; what's happening?" I inquire.

"Well, the Cerberus are closing in. Cato has tracked them to the top of the state; they should be here tomorrow night," Isaac confirms.

Cato agrees. "It is true the Cerberus are nearing. They have been Embracing and feeding, so they will be strong, but the newly Embraced are childlike, unable to control their powers, and will be used as pawns."

My heart leaps into my throat at the realization; in this fight, we are about to face, we could lose someone. The thought is nearly paralyzing, but I try not to show my fear and remain focused.

We continue to discuss the newest revelations as Elijah calls Ms. Edwina to notify her and the girls.

"They are heading back over," Elijah says, also trying to conceal his nervousness.

Cato explains that he has a great power; he's able to render enemy powers useless. From what he tells us it's similar to Alexander's power, and he can pick and choose who it's directed towards. However, he's limited on how many powers he can disable at one time. I think this will be very helpful in combination with The Magnificent Ones and their potions and such. He agrees to stay and fight with us. He's pleased with the alliances we've been making and believes the leaders of the Renata will be pleased as well. This is turning out to be in our favor; I begin to relax. It seems like it will be an easy fight, but we still have no idea what the Cerberus will have up their sleeves and need to remain prepared. Someone from our group is bound to get injured.

Elijah formally introduces Cato to the Williams and their pack. I can sense a slight tension, but everyone here is on common ground. I think once we all learn to trust one another, even just a little, the tension shall subside. Isaac and Constance are discussing getting human blood from some donors tonight, but don't want to stray too far from town. I overhear them suggest some of the homeless down at the shelter. Cato still lives off human blood and doesn't have a day crystal, but he agrees to keep hunting to a minimum while he's here. Isaac explains to Cato that he'll go to the hospital tonight and begin to sneak out a little extra blood supply for Cato, as well as fresh donations that he and Constance will get. We've been trying to obtain fresh blood every other day since we began our training; to increase our strength. Because Cato is so old – he has been a vampire for over a thousand years, he's learned to be a daywalker, without the help of a day crystal. He needs to avoid direct sunlight and can only go out in extreme overcast, but nonetheless can go out during the day. We want to ensure he never gets thirsty while he is here.

Once introductions are done and feeding plans established, everyone starts to settle in and begins to get to know one another. Knowing each other a little better will make it easier to trust each other when we fight as a team. The shifter boys are extremely nice, and Dakota really seems into Ebony. She very quickly begins to talk about Matt and thanks Dakota for his flattery.

The Agawam tribe explains about their history, which I find extremely interesting. Their ancestors are said to have been involved in the Tansy wars, back in the late 1600's, when the Cerberus tried to take over the area. Every few hundred years they come up with a war to gain power and take down the Renata. The story explains that the Agawam tribe helped to rid the area of many Cerberus. It appears that we were allies even before we knew it and history is repeating itself. They're very well invested in this upcoming...fight, I really hope it doesn't turn into another war like Tansy. Vampire history proves the war of Tansy is the closest the Cerberus got to receive enough power to achieve their goal. The Renata came to New England in full force and lost some of their main leaders, but in the end still prevailed.

"Tamo, I must say, we're all very grateful to have you and your tribe working with us. We're becoming very attached to Wenham and will protect it at all costs," Elijah admits.

"This is our motherland, and it is nice to know there are others that want to keep it safe as much as we do," Tamo replies.

Elijah's always been very personable but there's something different here. I see a kinship building between these two men like never before. I may not be the only one building lifelong bonds in Wenham. I enjoy looking around our home and seeing so many friendly faces and not worrying about our secrets coming out because they know everything, and we know everything about them. I can't help but imagine that we're meant to stay forever, and happiness warms through me, like the sun feeding its energy into the Earth below. Then I remember what's coming and the peaceful feeling dissipates.

Starting to get anxious, I decide I can't stand to wait any longer…I have to see Nathanial. I don't want to be rude, as it is nice to make new friends and I want to mind my manners. I look at Alexander to inform him of my plan; he agrees that it is a good time as Cato's well involved in conversation with the shapeshifters.

“Thank you, everyone, it’s been so nice to meet and get to know all of you. I’m going to excuse myself for the evening. I need to be alone with my thoughts and prepare myself for what’s to come,” I announce.

Upstairs I take a shower and make myself presentable and a little less disheveled. I promised Nathanial that I’d come by tonight; I have to keep my promise, since my siblings and I will miss school tomorrow, and possibly the rest of the week. I need to make sure he knows what’s happening and that he remains safe; I have to see him. We won’t allow him and Matt up at the meadow again until after the fight, and the same goes for Danika. Tomorrow morning we’ll call the McCord’s and finalize arrangements for her. We’re assuming the Cerberus will be drawn to the clearing because Eliza supercharged magical energy around the area to draw them in.

Stepping out of the shower, I dress and braid my hair, I quietly leave for Nathanial’s house. It’s not easy sneaking out of a house full of supernatural beings that have super hearing. I guess I can be grateful for being so light on my feet. I don’t know how to tell Nathanial that tomorrow is the day. I want him to stay as far away as possible; I refuse to let him get hurt again. The Cerberus will already be bloodthirsty with the mortals that are fighting with us…it will drive them mad, and that may be the hardest part of the fight. I can’t imagine how difficult it will be for him knowing that I’m in the fight and he can’t do a thing to protect me or help us.

∞ ∞ ∞

Climbing through Nathanial’s open bedroom window, I make sure not to make any noise…I don’t want to wake his parents. I hate sneaking around like this; it makes it feel so wrong. Nathanial is sitting in bed, reading a book waiting for me. Once I get to his side he looks up and smiles, then reaches out his arms. I sit on the edge of the bed and prepare to tell him what happened after he left my house. With a slight pause, I nervously begin, “After you left we got some news regarding the Cerberus. They’re closing in on the area and maybe here as soon as tomorrow night. I want you and Matt to stay close to each other as we planned. Danika will come over tomorrow; she’ll attend school like usual with you and Matt. After school, she needs to come back here with you. Florence already cleared it with your mom but will confirm details in the morning.”

“Needless to say, I’m not happy about this, but I understand it needs to be done. I promise to stay away until it’s clear, and not to go out unless I need too and definitely not at night.” I hear the reluctance come out and can tell he’s practiced his response.

“I try to understand how this must make you feel, but my biggest concern is keeping you safe. I love you and have waited too long for you. I refuse to lose you now.” I look deep into his eyes, trying to see and feel what he is thinking. “I shouldn’t stay long…I need to feed tonight, and it must be fresh to ensure my strength.”

“So, feed off of me,” he replies bluntly.

“What are you nuts? What if I can’t stop?”

“Sophia, you’ve been feeding on fresh blood since New Year’s…have you hurt anyone yet?”

“No, but you’re different.”

“Why, because you have a taste for my blood? Won’t my blood just make you that much stronger?” he argues, “Let this be my way of helping. I’m not worried that you have my scent implanted since the night of my attack. Not to mention, I really wanna know what it's like."

He sits up behind me, his legs on either side of me, holding me from behind with more love than I could ever imagine. Gently he brushes my hair off to one side, and softly kisses the back of my neck. I feel tingles shoot through my entire body; I tilt my head back slightly, resting on him while my body weakens.

"Nate are your parents asleep?" I ask.

"They went out for the night; when I got home there was a note on the table. They're spending the night up at the mountain lodge," he confirms while squeezing me tighter.

We've never been completely alone in a house before, and I don't know if I can fight it anymore. Nate continues to kiss my neck and reaches around me, lifting my shirt over my head. His hands caressing down my shoulders and sides with such a loving touch, I melt further into him with every caress of his lips to my skin. He slowly stands up in front of me with nothing more than his boxer briefs on.

"Nate," I say with reluctance, as I stare at his beautiful body, perfectly rippled abs and broad shoulders. "I don't know if I can resist you much longer."

He slowly guides me back onto his bed, kissing my navel, and moving up until he reaches my pursed lips. I lift my head ever so slightly to reach his mouth; I can already taste the sweetness of his breath. I continue telling myself that I can do this; I can control my thirst for him. Arching my back, I press my entire body against his as our lips meet. He reaches for my legs one at a time wrapping them around his waist, and with me hanging around him, he repositions us on his bed, carefully placing my head on the pillow; he leans over and hits play on his stereo.

"Sophia, you're the love of my life, and I'm terrified to lose you. I don't want to go through life not knowing what it feels like to make love to you," he whispers softly in my ear.

"I love you too. I want this more than anything, and I'm just scared. We need to be careful, and at any time if I hurt you, tell me," I insist. "Sometimes I don't know my own strength."

"Don't worry, everything will be fine. I trust you," he says as he kisses my neck again and moves down my chest.

Is this really it? Are we going to make love for the first time? Every part of my body starts throbbing with passion, excitement, and fear. Nathanial's kisses get more passionate with every touch; we've always shared something special, but this is different. Tonight, I feel as if I can feel his every emotion; I feel his love and admiration for me and what I actually mean to him. Slowly lifting his head, Nathanial looks into my eyes and with a gentle ease, he runs his hands down my cheek. Moving his hand from my cheek down the side of my neck, he leans in for a kiss while sliding the strap of my bra from my shoulder. Running my hands down his muscular bareback, resting them on the ridges of his hips and pulling him closer to me I feel a sense of security.

It's happening as if everything is moving in slow motion; this is the most amazing feeling I've ever had, to be so close to Nathanial, to be one with him. With my eyes closed, I begin to enjoy the moment, the experience; and it is more amazing than I could've ever imagined.

∞ ∞ ∞

"I told you I'd be okay sweetie," he kisses my ear. "It didn't even hurt when you bite me."

"I'm so sorry…I couldn't resist, and it was only my love for you that stopped me. Your blood is the most amazing I've ever tasted! Now we need to be careful that nothing happens to you, and under no circumstances can you be near any vampire blood, or the Embrace will begin." I still don't really understand what happened. I assume it was the act of becoming one with Nathanial, sharing his blood while we made love. The exhilaration from having sex with my one true love must have increased my natural instincts and my senses to his blood. I know I was thirsty and he offered, but still, I shouldn't have bitten him. I place my hand over his wound and completely heal the bite marks as if nothing had even happened.

"How long will the venom stay in my system?"

"Only a few days, maybe a week at the most; it just needs to circulate, and your liver and kidneys will help to clean it out."

"I knew you could stop…I told you I trusted you," he says with a smile. "The connection between us that you drinking from me added, I just can't believe how amazing it was. I felt like for that brief moment we were truly one."

"You did? I was just so scared, not knowing what to expect from it. I mean, I've bitten people before, but it was nothing like what we shared; I've never felt like this before. It must be the amazing connection and love we share for one another." I lay my head on his chest and listen to his heartbeat. It's so fast like it's about to jump out of his chest, and I can smell every ounce of his blood pumping through each heart chamber. What amazes me most is that I'm okay with it… I'm not craving his blood. In this very moment I know I'll never hurt him because his love means so much more to me than his blood. I have finally found Heaven, and it's in Nathanial's arms. As we lay there in each other's arms skin to skin, just holding each other for a while, I begin to daydream again of what could have been if I was only mortal. We start to talk a little about our hopes and dreams for the future. "I'm so blessed to have you. My biggest dream is that we could be together forever."

"I know I promised not to bring it up again, but we can be. The power of our future is in your hand," he replies.

Is my family, right? Will I turn Nathanial? Because now more than ever I want to be with him forever, more than I ever thought I would.

"But....."

"Sophia don't worry about it now. Just enjoy the moment we just shared." He instantly calms me as he kisses my forehead.

I'll stay with him until he falls asleep; I can tell he is going to have a poor sleep. He's tossing and turning and keeps repeating the word 'NO' and 'I love you!' I leave a note on his nightstand explaining that I'll call him as soon as I can and to keep his cell close at all times. Reviewing the plan in my head, I remember that Nathanial and Matt will wait together with Danika; this might also keep them from coming to the clearing...we hope. If one wants to come the others should be the voice of reason. Florence called the McCord's earlier with an excuse about going away and asked if Danika could stay with them; of course, they agreed. Naturally, they wondered why Danika wasn't joining us on our little vacation; Florence just explained that she had a few important exams and an oral presentation. She told the McCord's that we had a death in the family and the trip couldn't wait, but since Danika is newly 'adopted' she didn't know the deceased very well, making it alright for her to be excused from the funeral. It really is the perfect story to cover our absence; although she's not one for lying Florence, does accept that it's for the best in some cases. She also added we will be helping with details and could be gone for a week or two. Mrs. McCord assures Florence that Danika would be well cared for and to take our time. I assume that is why they took off for the night; just for some alone time before having a bratty little girl in the house.

∞ ∞ ∞

Back at the house, everyone's still there, getting to know one another, with the exception of Cato and Tamo, who went to check the area together. It's nice; we've not been around others of the supernatural kind in many years. The Triggs family has since joined my family, I sneak in and join them back downstairs. Dakota is talking to Ebony; she seems to like him too, but only in a friendly kind of way. She is completely in love with Matt and I really doubt that anything will ever change that. I decide to join the two of them. Ebony knows me all too well already and can tell something is up.

"Sophia, do you wanna to talk about it?"

"Not right now, it can wait," I smile. "So, how's it going?" I ask, trying to ignore my concern for Nathanial.

"Not bad; is Nate tucked in all safe and warm?" Ebony whispers.

"Well he's asleep, but I don't think he'll rest till it's all over. He was tossing, turning and mumbling in his sleep when I left."

"I can't believe that you both date regular mortals and they're okay with all of this," Dakota interjects.

"Well I wouldn't say they are okay with all of it, but they're very accepting of us," I admit. "But we need to keep it on the DL…Cato can't find out. It's against vampire laws to have mortals knowing about us."

He smiles and nods with understanding, "It's kinda the same thing with us. Not really laws or anything, but we prefer to have others believe our ability is nothing more than a legend or myth."

We're getting to know Dakota and the other boys quite well, and they're all super nice. I can see some real friendships building here; we have a lot in common. I don't ever want to leave this town. I can't help but thinking that over and over in hopes that it can come true.

It's so nice to have friends that I can just be myself around without worrying about secrets and lies all the time. I've made some good friends over the years, but they never knew the truth about me and my family. I feel so different here like I finally belong. This is the happiest I've ever felt and yet we're on the edge of real danger; danger that even after more than a century I've never experienced, until now. This scares me, not because I'm scared of being hurt, or of the fight, but because I fear for those I care about. This town and these people help me to belong. I can't ask for anything more than the safety of Wenham's people.

Chapter 9

The Arrival

We're prepared for the Cerberus' arrival, although it's been two nights since Cato informed us they would be here. The animal pack or shifters as we have now come to call them, followed the Cerberus last night, gathering Intel. There seems to be about 25 members in total; they have not Embraced anyone since their arrival in the county. Tonight's the night, I think we're ready; we all remove our day crystals and place them in the safe in the office. We don't want to take any chances of the Cerberus getting a hold of them; that would be bad. Having our day crystals would give them the ability to be out during the day. We're hopeful that the fight will end before daybreak as they will also need to take cover. No vampire wants to burn in the sun; it's very painful. I have heard it's similar to burning mortal skin with hydrochloric acid. The shifters share what they've learned; that the Cerberus are sensing the power of the clearing and are heading that way. They'll outnumber us, but we're stronger, more knowledgeable and better prepared since we expect them.

I'm getting concerned again; they're too close for comfort, and I really don't want anyone in Wenham to get hurt. I knew that this was going to happen; I just never realized how emotional I'd be about it. If we just stick to the plan all should be fine, so I start to go over it again in my head; okay, we strategically situate ourselves around the clearing, so we'll surround them.

I decide to call Nathanial. "Hey hun, I can't talk long. It's time; the Cerberus are almost here. I just want to tell you I love you. Please make sure Danika stays with you and Matt."

"I love you too, be safe and don't worry; Danika's right here," he says with deep concern.

"'Kay, I'll call you as soon as it's over. Just don't leave your house for anything," I instruct.

∞ ∞ ∞

Alexander has us all connected telepathically so we can see and hear everything he does; we can also communicate throughout the fight. The Cerberus are closing in…we can sense them. Normally we can't sense other vampires but tonight we have the help of Alexander's gift. He's opened up to the area allowing their thoughts in; yet keeping ours safe and tight within our group. They're so hungry, ready for the kill, and ready to gain the powers of the area. I wonder how Alexander deals with the torment of others thoughts all the time.

"It's difficult, but I've had time to learn to deal with it. The Cerberus is horrible though. I've never felt anything like this before," he replies back in our thoughts. *"I'm just glad I only hear their thoughts and can block out their emotions, at least to a point."*

We can feel their hunger; it's so overpowering, really the only thing on their minds, and it's intense, making us gain the thirst for blood that they have. We need to remain focused and not allow their feelings and thoughts to implant on us. The hatred they hold toward the Renata is almost as intense as their hunger; their thoughts and plans to take down the Renata are relentless. The Cerberus plan to increase their numbers and powers, then take over the royal palace to lead the vampires and eventually the world. All intentions they hold are pure evil; we feel it right through to our cores. Alexander's capability of dealing with others thoughts amazes me. I've found a new admiration for him.

Alexander announces through our connection, *"I'm releasing the connection to the area, we know they're closing in. I can tell how difficult it is for all of you to deal with, and that could weaken us. I'll keep us connected and I will check in on them every now and then."* Alexander's ability to withhold and permit certain thoughts; he's mastered this over the past century. He has enough control that he can remain connected to them and us at the same time; yet filter out what he doesn't want us to hear: our own little censor.

Time to focus on the fight; it is almost time. Telepathically we review our plan of attack.

"Okay, so we lure them to the center of the meadow, where our Magnificent Ones will cast a spell to trap them inside the crystals that were laid out. It should hold like a jail cell until they can use the power removing potion. Cato, you can then render their powers useless?" Elijah projects to all of us.

"I can only render a few useless at a time, maybe a little more if they are weak," Cato replies.

"I think your powers will best be used to weaken the stronger ones further. At that point we'll attack; once beaten and injured enough the shifters can rip them to pieces and we will burn them, placing the ashes in silver boxes and burying them in various places.

Just to ensure there is no chance of repairing." Wanting to ensure there is no chance for return.

We all agree with Elijah and signal that we understand the plan.

Our entire group prepares as we hear them getting closer, taking our fight stances and covering every point of entry. It appears they are only steps away. I'm relieved they are here and not in town, now we need to destroy them. I fear anything happening to the town and the adrenaline increases as my protective instinct takes over.

"Is everyone ready? It is time!" Elijah says through Alexander's gift.

The Cerberus begin entering the clearing. They are awful looking, at least most of them; their hair's a mess and their clothing is tattered and torn and very dirty. We can smell the scent of death on them. They're evil looking. The best way to describe one of them, who appears to be the leader, is...well, he looks like a psychopath. He is speaking softly to the others.

"This is the place – I can feel the magic here. Someone's near, more than one. This shall be our greatest feast yet. Can you feel the energy? It is amazing," he says softly, with great excitement and authority.

The others begin joining him in the clearing, one by one. We continue to talk telepathically as the cult members draw near, not knowing that we too are vampires until it is too late, and they notice the difference in our heart rates from the others near us.

"Remain calm everyone; fight your urge to attack...we must stay with the plan. Wait until they all reach the leader, and then cast the spells, girls," Elijah instructs.

As they enter the clearing one at a time from various points as if to surround what they find, we start counting them, 28, 29, 30, 31...36, 37, and 38.

"My God they have 38! That's twice as many as us! We only expected 25; they must have not all been together," Constance notes.

"We can do this; they are not prepared for us," Florence encourages.

They appear to be confused by the heartbeats of the witches and shifters versus ours. They prepare to fight for the food, fight to win our friends…as if we would allow that to happen.

"Now girls!" Cato screams.

The three witches begin to chant...

With the power of air
We entrap thee
With the power of fire
We entrap thee
With the power of water
We entrap thee
With the power of earth
We entrap thee
So mote it be,
So mote it be,
So mote it be.

Ms. Edwina assists with the spell to provide extra energy, like a power boost.

The crystals surrounding us and the Cerberus begin glowing as bright as stars in the night sky. As each one of the Cerberus notices they are caught off guard and begin to scramble, they even begin to fight each other.

Ms. Edwina calls to the girls. “Girls, come here quickly, the faster you act the better,” she hands each of them a potion to remove powers.

We all take our spots around the circle but remain back from the girls slightly.

“As soon as the potion is thrown the entrapment spell will weaken and with every hit or pressure put on it, the shield will eventually break. We need to destroy as many as possible before the trap breaks allowing them access to our friends. Alright girls, on my count, 1, 2, 3....,” Ms. Edwina yells.

The girls circle the Cerberus and throw the potions trying to hit all of them. Now that the potions are thrown, the girls run for cover, and we can begin our attack. The shifters are all waiting slightly behind us, ready to stake and rip the injured Cerberus apart or to attack any that may get past us. I’m starting to wish we’d have thought of flaming arrows; that would have done the job all at once…one wood arrow to the heart and instant up in flames.

One after another we are physically beating the Cerberus down. The shifters are doing a great job ready to tear them limb from limb. Ebony and Eliza remain behind all of us throwing potions that help us, either to enhance our powers or to weaken the Cerberus more. Ebony’s power of telekinesis is helping her with her aim of the potions. During a fight like this it is hard to ensure the potion hits the right target, but with a moment’s notice, she is able to redirect it if for some reason the vial is coming too close to one of us. It’s only a few short minutes before the entrapment breaks. The shifters charge and swoop down to attack and tear the Cerberus to sheds.

We make our way through the newest wave of Cerberus; they’re very easy, almost too easy. They are like worms crawling across the sidewalk on a rainy day, slow and easy to defeat. Now it appears we're down to about ten, and the remaining Cerberus appears to be older, more knowledgeable and stronger; they know how to fight. We can tell their powers are weakened but they still seem to retain some. I assume this because they are hiding in the middle of their clan when the potions hit.

"We can do this. There are only ten left, now we outnumber them," Elijah encourages. "Keep it up, great job. Isaac behind you!" Another one snuck in from the bushes charging us, and the shifters do a quick sweep to see if they can find more.

Vampire to vampire we are outnumbered, but we have help off to the side if things get out of hand. Growls roar through the area like wild animals, as we go head to head with the monstrous vampires that threaten our way of peace.

Isaac's having a good fight but is matched well. When he sees a chance, he takes his fight mate down to the ground, jumps up and Eliza hits the Cerberus fighter with a stun potion. Isaac jumps on top, staking him with a broken tree branch. The shifters come in and begin to destroy the fighter, ripping his head off, followed by all his limbs. Isaac turns his attention to another fighter that begins to attack. Muay Thai style, he begins using all his kickboxing moves, with stealth Isaac moves punching and kicking. For a brief moment as I watch him I remember how he described the difference between Muay Thai and other martial arts such as Taekwondo, *'we break bones, not boards;'* I chuckle at the memory as I return my thoughts to the fight.

We're all still linked telepathically, and Elijah is struggling; his opponent's strong, he must be the leader. He needs our help; Isaac prepares all of us, and he shakes things up a little. Isaac uses his power to control the elements and causes a small earthquake, just enough to take the Cerberus off their guard. The ground begins to tremble, we take our stances and prepare. The grounds movement increases, the Cerberus appear confused… we attack. They're completely unprepared, caught off guard as we hoped. Instantly we take out another five, leaving four Cerberus remaining. Alexander interjects their thoughts; Elijah is battling the second in command. We now see that they'd all been protecting whom we believed to be the leader. But we now have the numbers to win.

The Cerberus members continue to protect their leader, looking for a way for him to escape. We need to ensure his demise, to ensure the safety of Wenham residents; more importantly for me, that Nathanial and his family remain safe. The shifters close in the perimeter as we fight, and The Magnificent Ones close the perimeter, even more, fighting within the crystal circle the witches created to trap the Cerberus. As soon as we take a few more Cerberus out, the wolves can destroy them, and Ebony along with her sister can repeat the spell to entrap the remaining fighters and the leader in the circle with us. This will leave them no escape and lead them to their impending demise. The shifters dive into the center so to help destroy the Cerberus.

Two more down and the shifters are taking care of them; the spell is cast and now we are trapped with the leader and one last fighter. Constance and Florence are injured, Florence has a broken leg and Constance has a tree branch embedded in her abdomen. I tend to them as the boys and Matilda continue to fight. Florence's fracture appears to be a compound fracture of the femur bone, and Constance appears to be doing alright. She tells me to tend to Florence first; she's positive no internal organs have been damaged. I can't believe how lucky she is, a little higher and we would have lost yet another family member we love. My healing of their injuries is complete in seconds. Because they are vampires and can self-heal, my extra healing just helps to speed the process.

Once their healing is complete all four of us girls take on the one remaining fighter, and with all of us, he is quite easy to defeat. The boys are involved in battle with the leader; he's a good fighter, but with Cato's help he no longer possesses his extra powers. Cato's ability to render his powers useless, but his strength, we can't take away. Alexander is being tossed into the crystal shield like a rag doll. Elijah jumps the leader from behind, tearing at his flesh; piece by rotting piece it falls to the ground. Cato punches completely through the leader's chest and he collapses helplessly to the ground. Cato tosses the undead heart off to the side and shakes his hand free from the blood it is now covered in.

As the boys rip him apart, the sister witches remove the spell shield. We begin tossing pieces of the last two Cerberus remains to the shifters, and they proceed to toss the pieces into the fire. Once all the pieces are burned to ash we put the large blazing fire out. We collect the ashes and place them in silver boxes Alexander and Nathanial made, and seal them. Gathering all the boxes, we bury them deep into the ground in various spots throughout the forest, taking no chances of a hiker finding the remains.

Now that the job at hand is complete we begin to celebrate; the shifters, the witches, and the vampires, what an awkward combination of allies. I can't help but wonder if our little group of supernatural's have come up with something here. Maybe those like us can choose to work together, an idea I may have to revisit at another time. We cheer and hug, then Elijah decides to say something.

“I’d like to thank each and every one of you for your assistance in handling the Cerberus. It couldn’t have been successfully accomplished without your help. We’ll be forever indebted to you all.”

Everyone continues with the celebration. Ebony and I decide to sneak off to the other side of the clearing. “I think we should call Nate and Matt. I assume they are going insane,” I suggest.

“You are probably right…not to mention that, as much as I have enjoyed Dakota’s company, I miss Matt so much my heart aches,” Ebony admits.

I push the speed dial on my phone to call Nathanial, and he answers on the first ring. “Sophia is that you?” he asks in a panic.

“Yes, it’s me. Are you doing okay?”

“You are asking if I’m okay? How’s everyone? Did anyone get hurt? Did you defeat the Cerberus? Where...”

“Stop! You can calm down, I’ll explain everything. The Cerberus are now destroyed and we’re all fine. Why don’t you and Matt meet us at my house? I guess you should bring Danika too,” I try to reassure him and make a little joke.

Nathanial will ask if he can spend the night, it’s teacher’s convention tomorrow, so no school. Matt will stay as well; we can tell them everything that way. I’m excited to see him but want to converse a little more with our little army.

Because of the kills, we could all receive a few new powers; normally we can sense our powers, but because most of us have never killed another of our kind we don’t know what it feels like to acquire new powers. Elijah, Isaac, and Cato try to explain it to us. Cato and Elijah will be able to explain which power or powers we’ve attained. Because we didn’t get a chance to witness their powers, due to binding them, we don’t know what to expect, and they both have the ability to detect others power. Due to the shifters involvement in destroying the Cerberus, I doubt many of us will get new abilities. We injured the Cerberus and the shifters destroyed them. From my understanding, we have to complete the destruction of another vampire to acquire their abilities or powers, but I really don't know much about it.

Cato and Elijah start explaining how when an immortal destroys another immortal their powers are gained by the one left standing. These aren't always good powers and to ensure proper usage of the new power they must be learned and controlled properly. With all of us there together it becomes a jumble of powers; Cato and Elijah are only able to make out the powers, not who they belong to. We'll have to figure that part out later, but for now, we talk about the new powers they sense.

"I want all of you to understand that some of the powers we are sensing are very powerful; they can be very dangerous because if others sense them they would destroy you for them," Elijah warns.

"We'll work with you to control them," Cato offers. They begin listing the powers. "We have sensed age shifting, appearance alteration, aura absorption, clairvoyance, danger sensing, pyrokinesis, and health optimizing/degeneration since the Cerberus arrived. These are the strongest powers we sense; not all the Cerberus will have had powers and younger ones wouldn't have developed them, so they could take time to discover," Cato explains further.

"Now there is also the fact of the shifters causing the final kill. I'm not sure if they will absorb the power if it will just be like normal like it is for us. We'll determine later if any of us acquired new powers tonight or not. I also find myself wondering if the power just stays in the area for any entity that requires these powers, or if no one is getting the credit do they just reabsorb into the earth," Elijah reinforces.

Well, this is all very exhilarating and no one knows what to think. We're happy to destroy the Cerberus and protect the people of Wenham, but it isn't pleasurable to kill another, no matter how evil they may be. We've sworn against violence and try to live that way; if not it would likely lead to the temptation to kill innocents.

It's been a long night and the boys are meeting us at the house. Alexander and Isaac suggest to Cato that they go scouting to make sure no other Cerberus are around the area. "I'll go, please go home with your clan...or family as you call it. I'll suffice alone," Cato offers. This is perfect because we don't want him to know of the mortals knowing our secret. He'd insist that they be destroyed, or he could destroy us for breaking the first law.

Chapter 10

Security

With Cato away, it's safe again for the boys to come around. Cato said he'd spend a few days scouting up and down the coast and call us nightly to report. If he finds nothing in a few days he plans to return home to Transylvania. This will be great; we haven't spent quality time with Nathanial and Matt in a few days, and now because of a day off school we have a long weekend to see them before we return to school.

Nathanial and Matt are already waiting at the house when we arrive, and Ebony and I can't get to their open arms fast enough. I try not to run to him with my super speed but do crash into him a little hard. It's wonderful to be wrapped in Nathanial's arms again. We have been inseparable since we started dating even though it has only been a few days since we saw each other, and even that seems too long. I let out a sigh of relief as he squeezes me tighter. He smells so good, I'm not sure if it his cologne of body wash, whatever it is I missed it. I turn my head towards his neck a give him one soft kiss, just below his facial hairline.

We all head inside. It's nice to be home with a sense of relief following us. We go into the family room, lighting the fireplace before getting comfortable. Nathanial and Matt are both anxious to hear all the details of the Cerberus fight. Even more, they want to see it through Alexander's eyes, through his memories of the fight.

Alexander relaxes and begins to show them as the rest of us watch their reactions. They don't quite react the way we had expected. Typical boys...it's if they are watching the best action movie ever made, or the Super Bowl. They're on the edge of their seats jumping and punching the air. Ebony and I can't help but laugh…they're so cute.

Once Alexander is done showing them every aspect of the fight the boys jump to their feet cheering, high fiving, and chest bumping as if we just won the big game. "Whew! That was awesome, they never saw it coming! Man, I wish I could have been there," Matt shouts.

"You're all okay though, right? I saw that Sophia had to heal some of you," Nathanial says with concern.

"We're fine and it is all over now," Florence reassures.

Danika congratulates us, but I can see she is upset about something. I assume she's only pouting about not being a part of the fight. Why does she have to be so childish all the time? Can't she realize it's not all about her, all the time?

I can feel Nathanial's hand trembling undermine. "Nate, you worry too much; really this should prove that we can take care of ourselves," I insist.

"I can't help it. I found you and have become extremely attached to your entire family; I feel the same as I would if you were all my own family. I never expected anything like this nor did I want it, but here it is, and I never want to lose any of you," he babbles.

Elijah walks over to Nathanial and sits on his other side. “Nate, we feel the same way about you. However, we can protect ourselves; we have for over a hundred years, more for some of us. Now you need to let us protect you and your family. That’s why we had to do this, to keep the townspeople safe.”

“I know. I just can’t help it. It’s in my nature to be a protector. I’ve always wanted to help and protect the ones I love. It’s just like my mom and wanting more children. Completely different scenarios in one sense, but in the other sense, they’re the same. I feel completely useless and helpless when it comes to her, and the same when it comes to your family,” Nathanial sighs.

“Nate, I know you feel responsible for your mother not being able to conceive again, I just never knew how much it bothered you. I might be able to help your mother,” I suggest.

“I couldn’t ask you to do that, it would blow your cover.”

“Not at all. I can do something like that so easily. I would sneak in and do it while she slept, or I could hug her from behind and just touch her abdomen. There’s lots of ways I can heal her, and no one would know anything, she would just end up fertile,” I explain.

While Nathanial, Elijah, and I discuss this matter everyone else is abuzz with celebrations. Florence join our conversation, “Now’s not the time; you don’t want to do something like this without making certain that they still want another baby. Nate will graduate next year and leave home. The McCord’s may be ready for their empty nest; they’ve had many years to deal with infertility. I just think this should be looked into first. For another thing, we need to celebrate tonight; we’re all okay, and aren’t in danger anymore.”

As everyone’s laughing and enjoying being back together, Nathanial and Matt fill us in on the school gossip. It’s only been a week since we've been in school, but the rumors that are flying are so funny. The entire student body is assuming that Nathanial and I split up; he informed them that we just went on a short family vacation, no need to elaborate any further.

After a few hours of chatting away, we all decide we need to have some downtime. Ms. Edwina and Eliza return to their manor. Ebony and Matt are spending the night here; we have several guest rooms that they can stay in. I think everyone just wants to be alone with their loved one; I know that's what I want. Nathanial and I haven't seen one another since we made love for the first time and I'm longing for him; I long to be held in his arms and hold him in mine. To feel him next to me will prove the fight is over.

Nathanial and I agree that we want to go for a swim; we grab some suits and head to the indoor pool. Turning on the stereo, we run towards the pool, jumping in cannonball style. I think every window in the pool room gets hit with the splashing water. We goof around and splash playfully and just having fun. It's perfect and very enjoyable, just the two of us, two people in love enjoying our time together. Nathanial is so incredible, his perfectly chiseled bodice dripping with the water, and his hair wet and all slicked back. I didn't realize how much I missed him over the last few days. I was so involved in the fight I didn't have time to realize my feelings; he was always on my mind, but I was preoccupied. Now I have him all to myself and I'm not about to let him go. I swim over to him and wrap my arms around him, holding him so close, feeling like I belong right there in his arms. I've never felt the need to be protected but have the most incredible sense of safety in his arms; it's perfect, just the way it should be.

After swimming we relax in the hot tub for ten or fifteen minutes; it's just the right temperature at 104 degrees. Sitting side by side, his arm wrapped around my shoulder and my head resting on his, my legs draped over his lap. We don't say much…there's no need to. Just being together, that's all I need. I can tell that it's all he needs as well.

Getting out, we help one another into the softest robes you can imagine. We head upstairs to my room; I have the urge to talk, normal kind of stuff, so I pull out my scrapbooks and pictures. "I want you to know so much more about me, so I think it is time to show you my life in the last century or so."

"That's great! there is so much more I want to learn about you."

We spend the next few hours going through all my pictures; I don't have any from my life before the Pierce family, so we start where my life as I now know it began. I've only a few pictures from our first days in Italy – we were very busy and left shortly after I was Embraced.

"These are amazing; I would love to go there one day. Have you ever been back?" Nathanial asks.

"We've been back a few times; most recently was in the 1980's. We lived there for a few years. It was nice, but we felt too much pressure from the Renata; they wanted us to join them and lead the vampires that occupied Italy. We wanted to follow their traditions but also wanted to be free; they still feed from humans and that is not how we want to live, so we left again," I explain. "I don't think it is that easy to move on with your life once you have joined them either. It is kinda like a monarchy; if you are born to receive the throne one day, you have no other life. All your choices are made for you. It's the same if you join the Renata."

We flip through all the pictures, life and times. Nathanial asks questions about where we were and how I enjoyed it, and everything seems very normal. We go through all the years and continents as if it had all happened in only a few years, the only difference being that I didn't age; sure, the styles changed, but I always remain the same. Nathanial makes a crack about the pictures being from a carnival where they dress you up and take an 'old time' photograph. I guess it is kinda what it looks like.

I find it so revitalizing and relaxing to finally share this with someone. I can't wait to sit down with Mrs. McCord and go through all of Nathanial's baby books. To see his life through their eyes would be amazing. I know how much he means to them. To see him grow up through his mother's eyes would be miraculous experience. A mother's love for her baby is something I will never get to experience. Due to my super healing as a vampire, if I were to ever get pregnant my body would reject the baby as if it is a foreign object or an invasion, like a disease. I suppose male vampires can reproduce with mortal women, but not the other way around. I don't believe anyone's ever tried, so immortal conception is kinda a mystery. I have no idea what would happen to the baby either, a half mortal, and half vampire baby. I shake off my thoughts and watch Nathanial as he flips through each and every page that now documents my many years. His eyes just light up! I'm amazed at how me being a vampire truly doesn't even faze him. He loves me for me and I still can't believe it. I'm truly the most blessed creature in the world.

Once we finish perusing my scrapbooks we decide to go see what the others are up to; neither of us wants to sleep…we need to make up for the few days we spent apart. Downstairs, everyone's just relaxing and enjoying the downtime. Ebony and Matt join us as we go to the art room. I decide it's time to show those closest to me my other love...the arts.

They each take a seat and I grab my guitar, and once I get it perfectly tuned I begin to play for them. I start by strumming mine and Nathanial's song, "Never Gonna Be Alone" by *Nickelback.* They appear blown away. "Sweetie that is awesome; I knew you played, but I never expected that!" Nathanial praises.

"Thanks, but that one is easy."

"I bet you kick butt at rock band. You'll never beat my high score," Matt jokes.

"Is that a challenge? 'cause you're on mister." I put his challenge to the test.

From there we head over to the entertainment room, and I get everything set up. "Let's see how you do at 'Band Hero' my friend."

"Great, I want the sticks," Matt shouts.

"Can you sing sweetie? I can play the guitar, but my voice would kill small children," Nathanial laughs, passing me the mic.

"Sure; Eb, do you want to sing or play bass?"

"Bass all the way, I'm with Nate on the killing small kids if I sing," she laughs as she grabs the controller and instrument.

Matt picks a song and sets it to expert for his drums. Nathanial and Ebony both go with the medium level, I also choose expert. "Okay, let's rock this joint," I joke while doing a little impersonation, banging my hand through the air.

Everyone starts playing and when it's my turn to start, I belt out every note in perfect tune and pitch. They all stop playing and their jaws drop. "What? I didn't think I was that bad," I defend myself, having this overwhelming feeling of self-doubt or embarrassment.

"No, it is just the opposite. We had no idea you could sing like that," Matt mutters to get the words out, still in shock.

"You have the most beautiful voice I've ever heard," Ebony adds.

"Yeah, I have nothing to say...everything about you is amazing," Nathanial says in awe. "But of course, I always knew you were perfect although a little clumsy from that first day when you ran me down in the hallway.

"Well in case you all forgot I'm a vampire, and we're perfect at everything, after all, we have years to perfect it. So, can we get back to the game? Oh, and I'm not clumsy…I'm just coordination-challenged," I laugh. "And Nate, don't think I missed that comment about running you down, mister." I playfully kick him in the leg.

We continue playing, having a blast, laughing and such, taking turns on various instruments. Nathanial and Ebony aren't nearly as bad on vocals as they had made out. This is what friends should be doing together on the weekends, not fighting evil vampires.

After we finish almost all the songs we decide that maybe it's time for bed. Ebony and Matt each go to their separate rooms and Nathanial follows me to mine. I duck into the bathroom to change into my PJ's and then crawl into bed beside him. He plans to sleep in his shirt and boxer briefs. I snuggle into him just like I always do when we cuddle, kiss him goodnight and we lay back to watch a movie. Nathanial's out almost instantly; I'm pretty sure he didn't sleep much the whole time we were out of contact. Tonight, I'm here in his arms and we both know the other is safe from harm. It doesn't take long before I'm out like a light as well, not realizing how exhausted I am from the fight and all the emotions that came with it.

∞ ∞ ∞

Morning comes, I let Nathanial sleep a little longer. Downstairs, I go into the kitchen to put some of those culinary skills Florence has taught me to use. I make hash browns, bacon, pancakes, and eggs for our mortal guests to enjoy. Back upstairs I wake Ebony, Matt and Nathanial to all come down for breakfast.

"Wow, Sophia where did you learn to cook? It's not like you need to or anything," Ebony asks.

"Hey, it is just a basic life skill; you never know when the ability to cook will come in handy."

I assume I've done a good job because they finish it all. Everyone takes turns in the showers and dresses for the day. We decide it will be fun to head up to the mountains for a day of skiing and snowboarding. Elijah, Isaac, and Alexander are already loading up all the necessary equipment.

Eliza shows up all ready to go, and since Luke came up from Harvard for the weekend, he'll join us as well. Eliza and Luke run straight to one another's arms the minute their eyes meet. It's so nice to see that they're still becoming close even though they have a little distance between them, with Luke going to Harvard. In the short time since our New Year's party where Eliza and Luke met, they've been speaking and growing closer every day. Luke always comes home for Sunday dinner with his family and Eliza has been joining the McCord family as well, giving them a little time together the past few weeks.

Once we are finally ready we leave for the ski hill, and it turns out to be another great day. This is a total blast, with the warm January air and relaxation the snow brings us. Who could ask for more? When everyone else is preoccupied, our family decides to take a quick run down the back side of the mountain, for just a little out of bounds fun. It's nice because we find some great mountain animals to quickly feed on. No one even realizes we were gone since we beat them all to the bottom of the hill. What a great day with family and friends. I wish life, or the afterlife could always be like this.

Today really reminds me of the last place we lived, Banff. It's a beautiful little town nestled right in the middle of the Rocky Mountains. I loved it there. The streets were always full of tourists and the most amazing music scene. Lots of people are transients of sorts; not homeless but passing through. They get jobs, live there for a short time and then move on to the next place. I hope to go back there sometime, and even more so I hope to share the beauty of the area with Nathanial. He'd love it there; the clearest lakes, the tall snow-capped mountains, and full green forest. Who wouldn't love it?

Continuing the day with all kinds of winter fun, we have hot chocolate at the chalet, snowball fights through the mountain trees, and just enjoy everyone's company. It's all very normal…we even run into a few other students from school who decide to join us for the remainder of the day. They're very nice and it's a ton of fun getting to know them better; it's different interacting with so many people though. I'm not used to being around so many mortals all the time; just another thing I'm enjoying about my new life.

Once we finish at the ski hill we figure it will be nice to take our close friends for dinner. Luke and Eliza offer to go pick up the McCord's and Ms. Edwina to join us. They seem excited for the ride as it gives them a little time alone together. The rest of us stop at home to change and will meet them at the restaurant for a great night out with close friends and family.

Chapter 11

Deception

I sometimes find it hard to believe what a wonderful group of people we've found here in Wenham. For us, a family of vampires, to have the ability to enjoy a meal in a restaurant, with an entire group of mortals, amazes me. Now I finally have some alone time with Nathanial, and I think he might actually stay awake tonight. I just feel like it has been forever since we just chatted, even though we've been together. Last night was downtime, tonight is us time.

"I can't believe how much I missed you during all this."

"Me too gorgeous, but it is finally over, and things can go back to normal now. I don't know if I'd have lasted another day with Danika."

"What did she do now?" I question with a hint of frustration.

"I don't…well I…she kissed me," Nathanial stammers.

"SHE WHAT? I'm gonna freaking kill her!"

"Sophia, it's okay. I'm pretty sure she got the hint this time."

"Yeah well, I'm gonna make sure she got it."

“It meant nothing. You’re the only one for me,” he tries to calm me.

“I’m sure that it meant nothing to you, but that isn’t the point. What the hell was she thinking? She knows damn well that we are a serious couple. Real smart way to get me to trust her…I mean, I always knew she had a little crush on you, but to kiss you?” I rant and storm out of my room on a mission to beat the living hell out of Danika. While normally light on my feet, tonight I storm through the house like a herd of elephants.

“DANIKA! Where the hell are you?” I holler.

Alexander comes running out of his room, “Sophia, calm down. Killing her is not going to solve anything.”

“Alex for once mind your own business, this is between me and that little bitch. I knew she was trouble from day one!” I yell with such anger and passion.

Nathanial is hot on my heels trying to calm me, however unsuccessful he may be. The rest of the family comes to see what the racket’s all about.

“What on earth is going on here?” Isaac asks rhetorically. Finally, I see Danika laying on the sofa in the family room, watching TV and obviously pretending not to hear me. She does a little stretch and glances over her shoulder at me only to turn back to her program. With one swift motion, I grab her by her neck yank her to her feet.

With attitude, she yells, “What the heck is up your butt Sophia?” Breaking free from my grasp, she steady’s herself.

“Like you don’t know; would you care to explain why you seem to feel entitled to kiss my boyfriend?”

“I…I…I’m sorry,” she stutters, slowly inching further away from me.

"Sorry? It never should have happened! Do you see why I can't trust you? You have zero respect for anyone; not me, not Nate, not even this family."

"Oh, Sophia get over it, it's no big deal. Honestly, just let me explain."

"There is nothing to explain, you crossed a line here and I'm so done with you." I feel my features begin to change as rage takes over…first the burning in my eyes and the ache in my jaw. I can't restrain myself any longer; I'm going to kill this girl. At the same moment Alexander reaches for me, I lunge at Danika, tossing her to the ground. One fist after another I punch her square in the face, each hit bringing satisfaction. Blood spatters from one side of the room to the next. With one fist tangled in her short mess of fire red hair, I slam her head to the ground. Lifting my arm and tightening my fist I prepare to strike her again. Elijah, Alexander, and Isaac pull me from the beaten young vampire and restrain me. Florence and Constance move in to help Danika.

"Will you let me go? I want to deal with this once and for all." I pull and push, but even my strength is no match for the two older male vampires. Through my peripheral vision, I notice Nathanial and I can see the terror and what I perceive as disgust on his face. Immediately I begin to calm down, feeling the features of my face retracting, embarrassed and ashamed that he saw me in all my primal rage. "I'm fine, just keep her away from me for tonight; we can deal with this in the morning. I do hope that someone will discuss the issue of her behavior with her…I can't promise I'll stop next time." I push the boys off of me and race back to my room.

Still furious and ashamed that I acted no better than her, I pace back and forth in my room, afraid of what Nathanial thinks of me now.

How am I going to fix this? He is always going to see that awful monster every time he looks at me now. A soft tap on the door interrupts my thoughts, "What?"

Slowly cracking the door open Nathanial peeks in, and I turn away, unable to face him.

"Sweetie, may I come in?"

My heart leaps…he called me sweetie! *He doesn't hate me or is he just treading lightly 'cause he's scared of me?* "Of course, I'm so sorry Nate. Can you ever forget what you saw and forgive me for acting like that?" I ask, nearly begging.

"Come, let's sit down." Walking towards me, he takes my hand and leads me to the edge of the bed. "I have to admit I was shocked to see you react like that, but in all honesty, if someone else kissed you, I would've done the same thing. So, you have nothing to be sorry about."

"But I do; I'm sorry you saw me like that, that I lost complete control and I'm sorry I was such a bitch earlier."

Raising his hand to my cheek and turning me to face him, he said, "Sophia, this is my fault. I should have waited to tell you. You're just coming down off the fight with the Cerberus and your emotions are still raw. I just should've waited."

"No, you did the right thing, I'm glad you told me."

"But if I'd waited maybe things wouldn't have gotten so out of control. ….Who am I kidding, you have been looking for a reason to go at it with Danika for as long as I've known you. You would have kicked her ass no matter when I told you." He chuckles a little and pulls my head to his shoulder. "Now I can think of something better to do than talk about your bratty little sister." He flashes his crooked little half smile and pushes me back on the bed as he begins to press his soft lips to mine, with even more love than before.

Chapter 12

Danika Escapes

After Constance and Florence help clean me up from the beating Sophia laid on me, I go to my room, devastated that she didn't even give me a chance to explain why I kissed Nathanial before she attacked me. The past 18 months since being Embraced and becoming a vampire have been trying for me…being fifteen for all eternity is going to suck. I would've been nearly seventeen by now, starting to drive, finding someone to love. That was all I wanted to do, to find out what I was feeling. I mean, how could I be sure if I have never even kissed a boy before? I never wanted Sophia and Nate together; I hurt inside every time I see them all huggy and kissy. I never knew what I really wanted, I just wanted to belong. Well now I've kissed a boy, and I know for sure what it is I am feeling. I'm not in love with Nathanial; I'm in love with Sophia.

With this new realization, I know that I can't stay here any longer. Picking up my phone I decide to call Drake. I think it might be time for me to return to Club VC and become a more active club member…time to party a little. Drake has always been kind and urged me to live as a true vampire, not like a pansy vamp as he calls it.

“Hey Drake, it’s Danika.”

“Hi kid, you ready to come and party with me again?”

“Yeah, but I have to get out of here and…well, do you know where I can stay for a while?”

“My apartment’s just above the club; you’re welcome at my place as long as you need. Want me to come grab you?”

“That’d be great, thanks. I’ll escape through the forest and meet you at the edge of town.”

“Perfect: we’ll head straight back to Boston. Will an hour give you enough time?”

“Yeah, and thanks again, Drake.”

“No problem kid, you know I wanna hang with you a little more.”

I set the phone on my desk and shuffle through everything looking for my notepad. I know they were worried last time, and I don’t want them coming after me. I’ll explain it all and hopefully, they will forget about me the way they did with Caspian.

January 28

Dear Pierce family,

Thank you so much for everything you have done for me, but I feel my time is up here. Your family is so amazing, and I am only causing trouble for all of you. I will stay in contact when I can. You trained me well, so please don’t worry.

Sophia, I want to explain about me kissing Nathanial. I was feeling extremely jealous about your relationship with him and wanted to test those feelings. For me, this test was a success. I don’t have feelings for Nathanial...I have feelings for you. I thought I was confused, but kissing Nathanial gave me a sick feeling and I knew for sure. During the short kiss, I found myself wishing it was you I was kissing. Yes, you are reading this correctly, I'm a lesbian. It's because of this revelation that I need to leave. I need to find out who I am before I can be a part of this family. I know we have our share of differences, but I love you all.

Please, don't worry about me. I'll be fine.

X. O. X. O.

Danika

∞ ∞ ∞

Leaving the note on my bed, I sneak out my window with a quick glance back, then run to the road where Drake will meet me.

"Hey, kid, get on in," Drake greets me.

"Thanks, Drake. I just can't stay here any longer." A single tear trickles down my cheek.

"I'm glad you decided to come hang with me."

I give him a small smirk as we head down the interstate to Boston. Drake takes his time and drives only the speed limit as I stare out the window with not much to say. The Pierce's are a great family; I just don't think I belong with them.

Before long, Drake pulls into the parking garage at his apartment and we take a secret entrance down to Club VC. The stairwell is narrow and dark, only lit by small lights embedded within the stairs. A second door opens and the bass booms through the opening into the stairwell inside the club. Black lights shine down, and the smell of blood is overwhelming. It looks as if there are hundreds on the dance floor, bobbing to the electronica music. Probably a good mix of vampires and their human minions that have been compelled or hypnotized to do as their master wishes occupying the dance floor and VIP areas of the club.

"You look thirsty kiddo, let's get you a drink," Drake says as he grabs my hand, pulling me towards the bar. "Hey buddy," he greets the bartender. "One shot for the kid and a tap for me."

"Sure-thing Drake, this one's got an untapped vein right in her thigh. Go ahead and have at her. She is pretty tasty too," replies the man as he licks his lips and passes me a glass of deep red blood.

"Thanks, my name is Danika," I shout above the music.

"Is this your first time here, Danika?"

"Na was here on New Year's with Drake, but I think I'll be hanging around here a little more now. I don't really have any place else to go and Drake's being really nice and is going to let me stay at his place."

"Sounds great, and my name is Hugo, but everyone calls me Buddy."

"Why Buddy?" I ask.

"I man the bar, so I'm everyone's buddy," he chuckles.

I crack a grin; he's nice looking with a long black ponytail, full beard and he's fairly built. He's also got nice taste in girls – the one on the bar is quite a looker, but she'll probably be dead by the end of the night. I slam back the shot, tipping the glass upside down on the bar, and thank Hugo one last time before making my way out to the dance floor. Almost instantly the fresh shot of blood has a euphoric sensation over me. I try to forget my problems and the fact that the woman I'm pretty sure I'm in love with just kicked my ass and hates me more than anything. A sense of panic takes over me. I can't see her ever forgiving me; will I ever be able to face Sophia, Nathanial or the Pierces ever again? My God, I wonder what they all think of me now…how could I just leave a note telling them I'm gay? Will they ever let me back? I mean, they are all from another time then I am, and might not be as accepting of a gay person as others might be. Will others be okay with it? What will everyone at school say? Will they accept me? Has Wenham even had someone with a different sexual orientation than most? So many questions, and no answers; maybe I will never have the answers. At least Drake accepts me and is providing me with a place to stay. It's funny how I denied who I really am for so long, and now that I have realized my sexuality, I can't help but wonder how I didn't acknowledge it sooner. It feels good to want to be true to my feelings, so I guess it doesn't matter what others think of me. Shaking off my thoughts I try to forget all my troubles, if only for a night or two. I just need to clear my head, so I start bouncing on the dance floor with so many of the other patrons.

Chapter 13

Missing

Nathanial and I both awake to the sound of Florence's shriek followed by deep throaty sobs. Jumping out of bed, we both race out of the room to see what the commotion is. We find Florence kneeling on the floor of Danika's room, holding only a piece of paper as the tears stream down her face. Constance and Matilda are already there, trying to console her.

"What did the brat do now?" I question sarcastically.

"Sophia now's not the time for your petty little grudge. Can't you see Florence is upset?" Constance reprimands.

"You're right; Florence, I'm sorry. What's going on, where's Danika?"

Matilda gently takes the letter from Florence's hand, and passing it to me she explains. "Danika's run away, and I hate to say it Sophia, but it has something to do with you."

"With me? Why; just because I kicked her butt? Florence, I'm sure you have nothing to worry about. She'll be back soon."

"Just read the letter…she explains everything," Constance mentions, as she continues to comfort Florence.

Nathanial and I read the letter together and at the same time, we turn to look at one another. Complete and utter shock runs across both our faces as we look between one another and the letter.

"Are you kidding me? Now she thinks it's me she's in love with?"

"That appears to be what she thinks. I just don't understand why she thought she had to leave. I love her, no matter what. In such a short amount of time, Danika has become one of my daughters, and I would not trade one moment I had with her for anything," Florence continues to weep.

"Can I assume the boys are looking for her?"

"Yeah, they raced out of here as soon as we found the letter," Matilda adds.

Nathanial kneels next to Florence, and with his arm around her he helps her up to a chair. I've never seen Florence like this before, not even when Caspian left us. I can't help but wonder if what she's feeling now isn't just about Danika, but also about Caspian. Trying to think of something I can do to help I realize that maybe Ebony and Eliza can scry for Danika. Scrying is used by witches to search for something or someone. I've seen Ebony do this before and all she requires is something that belongs to the person they are searching for, a map, and the use of a pendulum which has been blessed and magically charged. This might work…I'm going to have to go and ask her right away.

"Florence don't worry, I have an idea that might work. I'll be back in a bit." I hurry out of Danika's room, and once downstairs I run out the door and jump in my car. It should only take me a few minutes to get to the manor.

∞ ∞ ∞

I call Ebony and fill her in on the situation as I drive over. As I pull up in front of the hundred-year-old manor both sisters, Ebony and Eliza, are on the front porch waiting for me. I bring the car to a screeching halt and slam the transmission into park, then race up to meet them; the sooner we can find Danika the less trouble she can and will get in.

"Did you bring something of hers for us to use?" Eliza questions.

"Yeah, I grabbed a scarf of hers as I ran out of her room; will it work?"

Eliza takes the multi-colored fashion scarf, "It should…have you seen her use it before?"

"It was one of her favorites; I'm actually surprised she didn't take it. Obviously, she didn't plan this."

Ms. Edwina walks up behind the girls. "Come in Sophia, I have everything set up. I created a circle already girls, just cleanse yourselves and cut a door."

We enter the family room and the magic circle is obvious by the candles Ms. Edwina has placed around the scrying mat and map of Massachusetts. Once a circle is created a door must be cut to enter and exit, and always closed after doing so to ensure that no evil can enter the circle. The two girls take their simple wooden wands that have a triquetra carved on the handle and a clear white crystal wrapped on the tip and trace an outline of a door in the air before entering the circle. The wand leaves a pale green mark in the air momentarily as they work; this shows how powerful the two sisters are. To be able to see the magical energy coming from them is unusual for most witches, but it's attached to The Magnificent Ones so strongly that we can see it with most of their magical work. I watch as Ebony and Eliza enter the sacred circle and the candles around them begin to grow bigger and brighter, feeding from their energy. The girls sit on opposite sides, one to the north and one to the south of the map, joining their hands over the area and closing their eyes. From what I've learned the girls have constant energy, to guarantee they get best results whenever needed. As the flames on the candles rise, both girls open their eyes slowly… almost as if they are in a trance. Ebony gently lifts the pendulum from the scrying mat as Eliza holds Danika scarf.

Together they begin to chant, "Take us to Danika, take us to Danika."

The crystal quartz pendulum is oblong and comes to a point at the end; the stone is flawless and attached to a thin chain with a small moonstone ball at the top of the chain. The pendulum begins to circle and move around the map; I watch every move it makes to see if there is some hint as to where Danika may be. Right when the pendulum starts to slow and give us some indication of where to look, it speeds again to a different area.

Ms. Edwina pulls her chair next to the girls. "Let me try to help…maybe just an extra jolt of energy will help find this girl."

The two girls and their Grams focus all the powers on Danika and her scarf that they hold. With one hand they each take hold of the scarf. Ebony holds the pendulum with her free hand, the small moonstone ball resting on the upper part of her hand as the chain hangs down secured between her index finger and middle finger. The other two witches place their free hands over Ebony's so that their combined power can guide the pendulum. The magical tool begins to circle again, a large even circle around Wenham. The three women close their eyes and focus all their powers on Danika. The pendulum slows and traces a straight line between Wenham and Boston, without giving us a specific location.

"I don't understand why we can't locate her," Ebony says, flopping down her hands down to her lap.

"Do we know what power Danika has yet?" Ms. Edwina questions with a look up at me.

Pacing back and forth on the outside of the sacred circle, I shake my head, "We aren't even sure if she has one. It's been over a year and a half and not one of us has seen anything from her, nor has she mentioned anything. Not even Elijah has picked up anything from her."

"Well, my dear, I think we have figured it out. With the three of us scrying for her, we shouldn't have even needed something belonging to her. The girls are so powerful, with my added power and experience we shouldn't have any difficulty. Yet we're unable to get anything definite."

"So how does that tell you what her power is?"

"Something is blocking her, or at least blocking us from finding her. I believe she has the power to shroud herself," Ms. Edwina informs me as they release their circle. She goes to her office and returns with the Book of Shadows.

"The Book of Shadows can't possibly have much information on Danika. Wouldn't you three be the only ones to make an entry about her? She is too new for any of your ancestors to have known of her." I remember when Ms. Edwina presented the girls with the Book of Shadows, it explains that the one who possesses it must enter any new supernatural information they come across. Since Danika is so young only Ms. Edwina or the girls could have done so.

"You're correct Sophia. But there is information on various powers our ancestors have come across as well. As you know powers are very much dependent on the person who holds them. We all know that even as a mortal Nathanial has the gift to get people talking, even if they don't want to. The Book of Shadows explains about a gift, called shrouding. This is the ability to hide from others. Those that possess this ability can also block other powers when it comes to them, such things as blocking Alex from reading or seeing their thoughts, or even you from healing them," she reads from the book.

"Aw hell, why couldn't I have that ability? I am so sick of my brother knowing everything I'm thinking and even sharing it with others. I'd love some privacy in my head," I joke and add, "That actually makes sense, cause Alex never has anything interesting to share about Danika. I guess this explains why; she only shares what she wants to with him."

"Yes, this could explain it," Ms. Edwina agrees.

"Hey Sophia, speaking of powers, have you all figured out what powers you gained from the big fight?" Ebony wonders.

"Yeah, there were a few, but mostly it was the shifters who fully destroyed the Cerberus. I think Elijah and Cato each got one, I don't really remember. I stopped paying attention once they confirmed I got nothing."

"You can be so pouty sometimes," Eliza teases.

"Girls pay attention here, we still need to find Danika," Ms. Edwina interrupts.

After a little more discussion, we decide to go back to my house and give the information to my family. It appears that Danika is somewhere between here and Boston. A bit of a big search area, but we can split up. In the car on the way back to my place Eliza calls

Luke and tells him that Danika's run away, explaining that we have reason to believe she's heading to Boston. She asks if he could check out some of the hot spots for us and he agrees. They've really built a solid foundation to their relationship since our party where they met. Matilda's even confirmed they are soul mates…of course, we're all sworn to secrecy as she wants them to have a chance to let it all play out on their own. How are we all finding our soul mates in the same place? I guess it just proves that fate handles certain things for us.

Chapter 14

Searching

At the house, Elijah and the boys have returned from their search by the time I arrive back with The Magnificent Ones. The entire family is in the family room now, still obviously trying to calm Florence, and they barely notice us as Ebony, Eliza, Ms. Edwina and I enter. I clear my throat, yet they don't even notice and continue with their conversation. Elijah is explaining that he and the boys found no trace of her; they weren't even able to pick up her scent past the interstate during their initial search.

"We have to assume she hitched a ride somewhere, knowing that we would find her if she stayed in town," Elijah hypothesizes.

I never even thought to try to find her scent. *Why didn't we do that on New Year's when she took off?* I wonder to myself. I guess it's only because we weren't as worried then; we know she is gone this time and that raises the stakes.

"Excuse me, I'm sorry to interrupt but we may have some interesting information for you," Ms. Edwina politely announces.

“Ladies, please come join us, I’m sorry we didn’t make note of your arrival.” Elijah helps Ms. Edwina to a chair. “So what information do you have?”

Ebony walks over and takes a seat on the sofa. “Sophia thought we should scry for Danika.”

“And?” the family all asks in unison.

I go and sit on Nathanial’s lap as we discuss the details of the scrying session and the probability of Danika having the ability to shroud or block herself.

Alexander bursts out with a huge smile on his face. “I’m so glad you figured out what Danika’s power is. Here I was thinking I’m losing my touch.”

Matilda smacks him on the arm, “Not everything is your business or about you for that matter,” She leans over and gives Alexander a kiss. “Darn good thing you’re cute.”

“Okay you two, can we please hear what else the sisters have to tell us?” Florence requests with despair.

“Okay so as I was saying, we believe she is somewhere between here and Boston. Eliza called Luke already and he’s going to keep an eye out for her, check out a few hot spots and such. We figure that he’s a good bet, since she knows no one else,” Ebony explains.

“Well, we should head to Boston tonight then,” Florence pleads.

“Florence my dear, I think we should search Danika’s room for clues as to where she might have gone. If she shows up anywhere near Luke, he’ll let us know. I just think we’re better off to go there prepared.”

Florence nods, “Come with me Constance, let’s start looking.” The two women leave the room and head up the grand staircase that circles around to the upper floor. I know Florence is hoping that Constance gets a vision of some sort.

Elijah leans forward and very quietly whispers, “Okay Isaac, now that Florence is gone, I want you to go online and use any other connections you may have to find out if there is any cult activity going on down in the Boston area. Check for businesses that look like they could be vampire owned. Let’s see if we can find where our baby girl has gone. I just think it’s too big of a coincidence that she disappeared right after the fight.”

∞ ∞ ∞

Back in my room Nathanial, Ebony and I wait for Matt’s arrival. I’m really starting to feel just awful about the way I’ve been treating Danika. She’s just a kid, after all, and has more to deal with than the average teen, and by average I’m not including any of our teenage supernatural friends. Since Danika first came into our family 18 months ago, I’ve done nothing but make her life a living or eternal hell. I give her a hard time about every little thing and criticize her every move. How could she feel comfortable here with me always insisting she is going to fail in one way or another? Nathanial takes a few large strides to my stereo system and puts on the music, I assume in an attempt to calm me.

Before long there is a rap on the door, Matt enters and walks directly to Ebony to hold her tight in his arms. “Hey guys, what can I do to help?”

“Everyone else has tasks to do, but we’re kinda just sitting here waiting for them to tell us what we need to do. I think we may get a trip to Boston out of this,” Nathanial responds.

"What happened to make Danika run away?"

Ebony smirks, "Sophia beat the crap out of her."

"What? You told her, didn't you? I told you it was no big deal and to keep your mouth shut," Matt lays into Nathanial.

"You know me; I couldn't keep it from her."

"Okay, wait a second, you told Nate not to tell me? Do you need me to kick your butt too?"

"Hell no, I'm good. I just didn't think it mattered. It was a small kiss and he pushed her away so fast. She felt so bad and begged him not to tell you…I just didn't think it was worth upsetting you over," Matt defends. "But I guess if the situation was reversed, I wouldn't be able to keep it from you either, Eb."

"You better not," she playful pushes him.

We continue to goof around a little waiting for someone to come in with information; I only hope they find out something. My heart is carrying so much guilt, it's all my fault. I reacted before Nathanial could explain. I refuse to let Danika say anything. Now with the extra information Matt just gave, I see it really wasn't a big deal. What have I done?

Chapter 15

Caspian's Surprise

Tonight I'm heading back to Club VC; now that my estranged family beat the Cerberus in their fight I have to try and find out what other plans are brewing. With my leathers on I'm ready to fit into the scene. Walking in the club I notice its busy tonight, but I already spot Cyrus and Drake. I can zone in on those two within seconds of walking in. With a crowd like the one tonight I bet they'll throw the sprinklers on. When it gets busy here I've heard they turn on a sprinkler system that sprays blood over the crowd. I think that would send most of these vamps into a feeding frenzy. Walking to the dance floor Cyrus stops me.

"Hey, Cas, nice to see you back here. You've chosen a great night to come; should be good times. We're planning some initiations tonight, care to participate?"

"Initiations, what's that?" I ask with slight caution.

"Ha ha, it's where we welcome new members into the group. They must prove that they are worthy and pass our test," Cyrus says with a demonic chuckle.

"Well, I think it may be something for me to consider, but we haven't known one another long enough, how can you trust me?"

"I just got a feeling, you're a good guy Cas, but nothing like making it official."

"I'll consider it, but you know me; I hate being tied down by responsibility to others. As I've told you I like to fly solo."

"Yeah I know, that's what I like about you," he smiles. "So, hey, I noticed Drake brought that young hottie you were talking to on New Year's. What was her name?"

"On New Year's? There were a few," I joke, knowing exactly who he's talking about… Danika. She must be back again. This isn't good if they are turning on the sprinklers and doing initiations tonight. I'm gonna have to stay close.

"The hot little redhead," Cyrus reminds me.

"Oh, what the hell was her name? Danielle? No, I've heard it before; oh, wait the same as that female race car driver, Danika. Is that it?" I try to play things down.

"Yeah, I think that's it. Maybe you should go re-introduce yourself. I saw her on the dance floor a little while ago. I'll catch ya later, got some work to take care of before the initiations begin." He smacks me on the shoulder and turns to leave, disappearing in the crowd almost as fast as he turned around.

I haven't checked in on my estranged family in a few days since their big fight, I wonder what happened that Danika's here. Maybe she just came to hang out again, but it can't possibly be a good time for her to be here. Tonight, they're going to try to get her to join them; what better way to get back at the Pierces than to take one of their own? I know Drake has had his eye on her for a while now, so I must keep my eye on him too. I notice Danika bopping away on the dance floor; she seems to be quite the popular item here. Just then she looks up and notices me. She bolts off the floor and over to me.

"Hey, you're Cas, right? Remember me? I'm Danika; we met on New Year's. Do you come here lots?" She rambles on like any regular teen, barely breathing between sentences.

"Yeah sure do. How you doing?"

"Great, I love this place. Everyone makes me feel so welcome; not like where I used to live."

Used to live? What does she mean? Oh, Christ has this stupid kid run away to come stay here? I gotta figure out what's going on with her. "What do you mean where you used to live? Your Embracer wasn't good to you?"

"I never knew my Embracer; he left me in the streets. I was taken in by a great family, but one of the girls, Sophia, who was like one of my sisters, had it in for me. What made it even worse is I have feelings for her."

"Oh wow, that sounds like a lot of drama. So how long are you staying here? Do they know where you are?" I try to gather a little Intel, so I can piece together a plan to save this brat. Wow, did Sophia have her pegged right? That girls got some killer instincts, and do I ever miss her.

"No, I didn't tell them where I was going, I just ran away. The family I lived with would never approve of a place like this. They try to act as if they're still mortal. I don't understand it though; this life is so exciting and cool."

"I'm sure they have very good reasons for the way they live; you know we're all different and this life isn't all it's cracked up to be. Do you know much about the people here? Cause I'll give you one bit of advice; when you're here and around these kinds of vampires, always keep your nose clean, and be very careful who you trust. They hold no loyalty to anyone but themselves and their king. The people that frequent this club will destroy you in an instant if they think it will help them advance." I try to warn her, but it starts to sound more like a lecture, and I notice her rolling her eyes at me. "Sorry Danika, I too am new here and just a little paranoid, if you know what I mean. Maybe we can watch each other's backs."

"Sure, just please don't try to tell me what to do…I'm so sick of bossy vampires," she lets out a small chuckle.

"I'll do my best; let's grab a shot and we can chat some more, that's if you want…you know I don't wanna be a bossy vampire," I smirk.

She smiles, "Great, you like dancing? 'Cause I'm having a blast out there."

"I'll give it a try. You kinda mentioned you were into chicks, right?"

"Yeah why, you got a problem with me being a lesbian?"

"Not at all, to each their own. I was just thinking we could be each other's wingman."

"Wingman, what's that?"

I try not to laugh at the naive girl before me. "We tag team the ladies, work together to help find someone to hook up with."

"Hook up with, wow…ummm, I don't think I'm ready for that yet. I mean I just realized that I'm gay in the past few days. I've never even kissed a girl."

"Oh sorry, I didn't mean to…well just forget it, we can just hang together. I'm just trying to act cool. Can I ask you something though?"

"Go ahead."

"Well, how do you know you're a lesbian if you've never kissed a girl?"

"I guess I don't really. I just feel it when I think of my so-called sister. I was always jealous of her relationship and thought it was 'cause I had a crush on her boyfriend. So, well, I kissed him, and it was disgusting. That's when I realized I was in love with her, not her guy. I mean, I just feel it. I think I always knew; have you've always known you were straight?"

"Wow, I bet she was pissed when she found out you kissed her boyfriend." I only assume knowing Sophia's temper.

"That's the understatement of eternity. She kicked my ass."

Uncontrollably I burst out in laughter. I can just see Sophia on top of this poor girl beating the crap out of her, storing all the pent-up energy from the fight against the Cerberus and laying it on Danika. "I'm so sorry. I really don't mean to laugh. You just don't seem like the type of gal who takes a good lickin."

"Well I did, but next time I'll be ready if there even is a next time. I left a note for my family and told them not to come looking for me. Even if they do, I doubt she'll come. Sophia doesn't give two…well, she just doesn't care about me and will be happier with me gone."

"I have a feeling you don't give this so-called family of yours enough credit. I bet they're looking for you as we speak." I know them too well and the whole lot of them is doing everything they can to find Danika.

"Well they'll never find me here, so I guess I don't have to worry."

"Maybe we should just try and have some fun, and forget about our problems for now," I suggest, trying to get her to forget about the

Pierces for now. I want her to need them back, not hate them after complaining about them. I know they have their flaws, every family does, but she really can't do any better than them. I should know…maybe we can go back together. Wow, I surprise myself, this is the first time I really thought of it as a real possibility. We get a quick shot and head out to the dance floor, with the plan of dancing the night away.

Chapter 16

Road Trip

Isaac calls the family and our friends into the family room; he has something to share with all of us…I think he may have a plan. Once Elijah, Florence, Constance, Alexander, Matilda, and I are there along with our two mortal friends and the witches, Isaac stands before us with a map of Boston.

"Okay, well I think we may have a lead on Danika. I know it's been several hours since she went missing, but I have some information as to where she may have gone. I found out about this vampire club in Boston. It's run by the Cerberus, although that fact is not made known to all the club goers. Tonight's their initiation night, and it seems they have their sights on a few new clubbers. I think Danika may be one of them. I've already contacted Tamo, he and the other shifters are already out scouting, trying to pick up on her scent or whatever else may be out there."

Elijah calmly says, "Great, I know the Williams family will do their best to help find her. Now, do you know what's included in this initiation? If we're too late, will we be able to get her back?"

“Not likely. The process includes the sacrifice of a mortal. Once you have done that you say a pledge to the leader. It is highly unlikely for him to release anyone that completes the process.”

“And is there any indication as to who the leader may be?” Constance asks with concern.

Isaac nods and chews his bottom lip; this is never a good sign. “My source claims it is Cyrus and his son Drake.”

Nate looks at me and around the room. “Who are Cyrus and Drake, and what does that mean?”

Isaac glances to Elijah and nods for him to explain. Elijah begins, “Cyrus is one of the original thirteen grandchildren of Cain, the first of our kind. He’s one of the few originals left today, making him the most powerful as well. Thousands of years ago, Cyrus was the leader of the rebelling grandchildren, and now the head of the Cerberus. Drake is his son; he has gone by many variations of that name. Draco was a former name, but he is most commonly known as Dracula.”

“Are you freakin kidding, like the real Dracula?” Nathanial says with excitement as he jumps from his seat.

“Yeah, like the real Dracula; or at least the one depicted to a point in the movies.” Elijah laughs and motions for Nathanial to sit down again.

“I heard that he may have been real, but never really knew for certain,” Matt jumps in.

“There is actually a long-standing tale about him and his demise,” Isaac adds.

Nathanial is nearly bouncing, “Well, don’t just tease us like that. You’ve got to tell us the tale.”

With a chuckle, Isaac begins, “It is said that Dracula was chased out of Transylvania. He fled to the docks and boarded a ship full of people that was headed to Whitby in North Yorkshire of the United Kingdom. Afraid of being found by those who were hunting him, Dracula transformed into a dog, as he has the power to shape-shift. Even as a dog, Dracula needed to stay out of the sun or he would burn, so he remained in the cellar onboard until night. Once nightfall was upon them, Dracula would transform back to his original form and find a poor soul to feed from, draining them to death. His only other option to feed was when a crew member entered the cellar.”

“That’s pretty cool; what happened next?”

“Back in Whitby, a couple saw the ship. Surprised as it had been so long since the last ship had passed through Whitby, they watched, wondering what was aboard. As the ship came to dock the couple realized no one was aboard the ship and couldn’t figure out how it was being steered. Now of course, with a little practice, vampires can control minds and inanimate objects; this allowed him to steer the boat with his mind. Once he disembarked the ship, Dracula realized sunrise would soon be upon him–he needed to find a safe place to hide out. Not far from the docks is Whitby Abbey; Dracula raced up the nearly 200 stairs to find solace within the Abbey walls.”

Nathanial’s intently listening to the story, “So how did he end up here in North America?”

“Once the people of Whitby found out about him, they hunted him and staked him. He was buried there at the Abbey. What the people didn’t know is he could be resurrected; because of his age and powers he was, and is, much harder to destroy. Dracula was staked, but not beheaded or burned, so he just needed a little help. It is said that his father Cyrus found him, as makers can sense their kin. He removed the stake and fed his son; not only mortals blood but his own blood as well, bringing Dracula back to the world of the undead. They left a tourist's bones in Dracula's place and staked the remains, making it appear that Dracula's body still rests in Whitby Abbey today. Only those of our kind are aware of the true story, and now you all share this knowledge."

"I assume that this is now a popular tourist attraction," Matt adds.

"You're correct son…many tourist go to see the grave of Dracula."

"Oh, I'm so there!" Nathanial announces.

"Now that's a very interesting story, but we have more important matters to deal with than a tourist attraction. I'm more concerned about, how bad is it going to be if they get their hands on– or should I say fangs in – Danika?" Eliza comically asks.

"Well-being that two of the most powerful vampires in history, I would have to say pretty bad. So, we better get going and get to Boston," Constance adds.

We decide to leave Ms. Edwina, Matt and Nathanial here, just for their safety and in case Danika comes home. With the remainder of us jumping in our cars, we race down the interstate towards Boston; at this rate, it should only take us about 15 minutes.

∞ ∞ ∞

In Boston, I drop Eliza and Ebony off at Luke's work and make sure they're set up. He's on tonight and explained to his boss that a friend of the family has run away to the Boston area. His boss is allowing the girls to use his office as a headquarters. No one questions why we have not contacted authorities yet, as there is a waiting period. No one there, not even Luke, is aware of all our supernatural connections, so the girls need to be careful not to get caught using magic. We're hoping that they'll be more successful scrying here since we believe Danika's in the area and the pull will be stronger. We're all armed with our cells and ready to go. Once Ebony and Eliza are set up in the office, my family and I are ready to proceed to the theatre district, where this club is rumored to be. We believe it to be below a mortal nightclub called the Bijou, as this someone suggested. Luke points us in the right direction and we speed off with urgency. Our only hope is that she hasn't gone through with the initiation yet.

In the parking lot of the Bijou, we notice several partygoers sneaking around the back; they're quick and the mortal eye wouldn't notice them or anything out of the ordinary. We are swift and follow them to the hidden door in the back of the building. Nodding with acknowledgment to the guard inside the door we begin to walk down the stairs.

"Hey, you guys are new, you got ID?" the burly man asks. Elijah begins to pull out his wallet. The man chuckles, "Not that kind of ID, the kind that will grant you access to our private club here."

We all laugh, and Elijah says, "Yeah of course man, sorry first timers here." Then Elijah flashes his fangs to the doorman.

"You got any regulars with you tonight?"

"Regulars? Oh, you mean…no, no, this is my clan."

"'Kay, just so you know you can bring regulars with you, but they require an armband, so they are marked. Red for free for all, meaning you can feed freely off them, and black for taken, meaning only their owner can feed from them. There's a bar inside – you can get a shot of freshly squeezed or you can get a tap. The selections for taps are presented on the bar and Buddy will assist you to find a good vein." He goes over the rules of the club. "And hey, enjoy Club VC; tonight's gonna be a good night."

"Thanks…we're just travelers looking for a place to fit in," Isaac plays along.

"Well, I think you may have found it, and if Boston doesn't float your boat, we have clubs all over and can hook you up with a chapter that will be to your liking."

"Thanks for the help." Isaac shakes the man's hand and we continue to make our way down the stairs to another door.

Inside the club, I'm shocked at what I see. Vampires are feeding freely off mortals and raving on the dance floor. I guess I've been somewhat sheltered since my Embrace, but I can't believe my kind would act this way in public. My biggest question is, how do they get the mortals involved? It's against all vampire laws.

Alexander connects us all and says telepathically, *"I assume they're all compelled or hypnotized to some extent. Also, don't forget we are amongst the rogue cult and they don't follow the laws set forth by the Renata."*

"Okay, try not to act too surprised by all this; we need to blend into our surroundings. Plus, we're here for one reason, to find Danika," Constance encourages us.

Florence hasn't been very talkative since Danika left. I know how bad she's hurting and want nothing more than to stop her pain.

"Well, I think we should split up. I've heard some of these partiers talking about the initiation. Florence and I will go to the east, Isaac you and Constance can go to the west, and Alex, Mati, and Sophia, why don't you go straight south through the dance floor," Elijah orders and we all agree. Alexander will keep our thoughts very

tightly connected. We must be careful, as we're unaware if there are any other telepaths here. Alexander will keep our thoughts on lockdown from others.

Alexander, Matilda and I all take to the dance floor, dancing and appearing to be having fun as we make our way through the crowd. I accidentally bump into someone. Turning around to offer my apology, I freeze as he turns to face me.

"Sophia, ssssshhhhh. I've got this under control. Get out of sight before she sees you. I'll meet Elijah in the men's bathroom in five minutes to explain," Caspian whispers and whips back around to dance with Danika, who thankfully had her back turned to us.

We duck out of the dance floor and Alexander calls the rest of the family to meet us by the men's washroom. Still, in shock Alexander and Matilda help me in the direction of the others. I just can't believe he's here, Caspian is here, and he didn't run. It feels as though my heart is in my throat. I can't wrap my head around what's happening right now. Caspian's here and has Danika. Is he a Cerberus now? My thoughts begin to race and the scent of fresh blood in the air becomes even more apparent.

"What the hell happened there?" Isaac runs to us. "Is it really him, is that really Caspian?"

Florence takes a chair in the corner; her emotions are visually apparent, and she, like the rest of us, is overwhelmed by the situation.

Caspian walks around the corner, "Everyone get in the bathroom, she's coming."

We all race to get through the men's room door in order to avoid being seen by Danika.

"Okay, before you all ask me a billion questions, I don't have much time, Danika can't be left alone for long. Drake and Cyrus have their sights set on her and you should all be careful; they know it was you that killed the others," Caspian begins.

"But…" I begin.

"Sophia, I promise we'll talk later, but this is about saving Danika. She's very hurt by the way you treated her. She feels like an outsider in the family. Now Drake's been working on her since you moved to Wenham. He's the guy you've seen her hanging around with at the school Sophia. Now on New Year's when she took off, she was here. That was the first night I met her. Tonight, they plan on initiating her into their cult. She needs to fully drain and kill a mortal, and then complete the Embrace on one of the taps. The taps are people chosen for live open vein feeding here. Right before initiation, the sprinklers go off, spraying blood through the sprinkler system. I believe this will start a feeding frenzy and begin the bloodlust. I'm keeping an eye on her, and Alex you can go ahead and connect me to all of you. There's a place you can go on the west side; the entire club is visible from there. I'll ensure that Danika stays on the south and east ends of the club. We'll talk more soon. Just remember, once the sprinklers start, it's go time, and we'll have to get her out of here if we haven't yet." Caspian says in a panic and slips back out of the restroom.

The seven of us stand there in total shock, unable to move or speak, just looking at one another and wondering if this really just happened.

Chapter 17

Danika's New Friends

Dancing with Cas is a blast, I'm so lucky to have made a friend already. I wait for him as he told me to, just outside the men's restroom. I'm glad to have him to hang with and to show me the ropes around here since Drake told me that his father had work for him to do, although he said tonight is a special night and will return later with a surprise for me. I can't help but wonder what it might be.

"Bout time...and you guys always say that girls take forever in the restroom," I joke as Cas walks out.

"Sorry, gotta look good; you know beauty like mine takes work," he jokes back. "Are you thirsty? You should make sure you don't get thirsty since they allow some mortals in here, and if you take the wrong mortal their master will destroy you."

"I could use a little something. I'm thinking of trying the tap, is it any good?"

"Probably not a good idea; have you ever had a live feed? I mean, you look pretty young and come off as a fairly new vamp."

"No, you're right, I've never tried a live feed; my old family didn't live that way. I'm wondering if there is anywhere safe I can try it."

"Oh, I'm sure Drake will bring you in here when it's not so busy. He should be able to train you to drink fresh."

"Who would've thought everything would be so difficult?" I complain a little.

I begin to feel a little pang for the family I just left. I'm so confused and don't know what to do. I'm having fun here, but some of these vamps are a little scary. The mortals they bring here are shocking…I think I heard someone call them minions. It's just hard to believe that they freely feed off them; some of the mortals are so out of it that they look almost like zombies. I wonder what they do to them when they are finished or get bored of them. A lot of the mortals appear drunk as well. I notice a small bar off in the corner that serves alcohol to the mortals; I've heard they're easier to compel or hypnotize when intoxicated. This is such a different life than I'm used to; I guess I never realized how much the Pierce family protected me.

"Hey Danika, you okay? You look a little lost," Cas makes note.

"Yeah, I'm fine, just thinking about how different this is for me."

"You know, it's not too late to go back to your home; I can take you."

"Thanks, but no, my so-called sister wouldn't want me to come back anyway. They're just better off without me. I've got a few issues I need to work out for myself too. I just don't wanna think 'bout this anymore, let's dance some more."

"You're the boss tonight, kiddo."

Just as we start toward the dance floor, Drake comes out of nowhere. “Hey kid, want the big tour? I can show you my office and stuff.”

“Yeah sure.”

Drake takes my hand and pulls me from the dance floor. Cas is right behind us following. Drake turns around, his eyes glowing bright red with a black ring around the iris, and looking right at my new friend he says, “Sorry man, this is a private tour, you understand, right?”

“Oh yeah, sorry sir…meet up with you in a bit Danika.”

“I’ll find you after, promise.”

Drake takes me into a back room, with his hands wrapped tightly around both my wrists; he pushes me up against the wall. “What do you think you’re doing with that joker?”

“I met him last time I was here; he’s just being a friend. Now let go of me.”

“You do not tell me what to do. I run the show around here and you will obey me,” he pushes me harder and presses his lips to mine. I try to fight him off, but he’s too strong for me.

“Drake please stop, I…I don’t like you this way, I like girls.”

“I don’t care what you like, I want you and I want you now.”

The door slams open and a larger, older man barges in. “Son, you let go of that poor girl, this instant.”

“Ah…yes, sir. Sorry, Dad.” Drake releases his grip from my wrists.

The man holds his arms open to me “It’s okay dear, come here.” His voice is filled with such authority. “My name is Cyrus…I think we briefly met last time you were here, young lady.”

“Thank you, sir,” I collapse in his arms.

"Please don't mind my son. He'll never do anything like that again. He has a little bit of a jealous streak, don't you son."

"Yes, sir…sorry, Danika. When I saw you with Cas I just couldn't help it. I really feel you are the one."

"She is the one?" Cyrus raises his brow to Drake and receives a slight nod in return before continuing, "Well Danika, tonight is a special night. We are initiating special vampires into our exclusive club and we would be honored if you will join us. It is like a large family; we will always protect you and make sure no one, including my son, ever hurts you again."

"Really, you want me? I'd love to join your club." I don't think I could say no if I wanted too. Cyrus has such a power over me, I have a burning need to serve him.

"Wonderful! Why don't you come to my office? Marci is in there and she'll help you find something beautiful to wear. In about 30 minutes, I'll come get you and we can announce it to the other members. I'll present you on the stage."

"That sounds wonderful; I feel like a princess or something."

"Oh yes, a princess; you are my little princess." Cyrus winks at me as he opens the door to his office and leaves, pulling Drake behind him.

The office is white…everything is white; the walls, the furniture, and there are a few paintings hanging on the walls, in white frames. It looks to be some kind of abstract art and only painted in red, almost as if to represent blood. On a white leather sofa, off to the side sits a petite woman; she is striking with long black hair and blood red eyes. Next to the sofa is an open closet, filled with dresses - also, all white.

“You must be Danika?” The high, yet musical voice rings out to me.

“Yeah, are you Marci?”

“I am, but I prefer to be slightly more formal. I am your elder, so you shall address me as Miss Marci.”

“Sorry, Miss Marci.”

“You know now so don’t let it happen again,” she demands as she rises from the sofa and begins to dig through the closet.

“Miss Marci, may I please ask how long you have been working here?”

“I do not work here. I’m Cyrus’s mate, his queen, and right hand. Together we rule; he as a father figure, myself as a mother figure.”

“My apologies, Miss Marci.” I feel the need to be very formal and proper with this woman. “How long have you been queen?”

“Cyrus and I have ruled for centuries; he found me and Embraced me. I have been by his side ever since, as a good queen should. Now will you stop with the silly questions; you need not concern yourself with my duties and history,” she snaps.

I’m a little terrified; no one’s ever been this intimidating to me before. She lays a few dresses out on the sofa. “Try these on.”

“Miss Marci is there a changing room?”

“NO, you will do it right here! I must get a look at what we are getting.”

“I, um, I don’t…”

“You don’t anything, young lady. Around here you do what you are told.”

“Yes, Miss Marci.”

I'm now terrified but try not to show my emotions as I'm sure I would just get reprimanded again; this lady scares the crap out of me. I proceed to disrobe and try on the first outfit; white leather pants and a corset style top, also in white. She points and instructs me to spin around with only a wave of her index finger. Then with one swift motion, she shakes her head and waves off the outfit. This goes on for the next five outfits. Finally, she gets up and swings open the closet doors, and after a moment of digging around she pulls out a white garment bag and hooks it on the door of the closet. Unzipping the bag reveals a long white silk gown.

"Here try this one; maybe it will look good on you," Marci snarls.

"Why do I even need to change?"

"You will not ask questions, girl."

"Sorry Miss Marci, it is very beautiful."

"Okay, enough talk; haven't you noticed I don't really care what you think? Now try on the dress."

I nod and do as told; no matter what she says I really do love this dress. It looks to be a replica of Pippa Middleton's dress from the royal wedding of Prince William and Catherine Middleton. I'm such a Royal fan, but never let anyone know or they'd tease me…at least I think they would. Right now, I'd prefer that to how I'm currently being treated. Before I can get too lost in my thoughts I'm instructed to spin again. Finally, she cracks a small smile and nods in approval. She then opens a large case filled with makeup and hair products and proceeds to do my hair and make-up. If she wasn't so mean and I wasn't so scared this might just be fun.

Chapter 18

Working Together

Caspian approaches us. "I'm quite concerned about Danika. Drake took her into the back and has since come out again, but she hasn't."

"Let me try to connect with her; if she is in danger or hurt, her guard might be down, and I may be able to get through," Alexander suggests.

"Good idea…just don't contact her yet. It may make the situation worse and we still don't know who can tap into our thoughts, or if someone else is already in her thoughts."

"Agreed."

We watch as Alexander concentrates. We can telepathically see him searching for her, and in moments his eyes open again.

"I can't get in, but I do sense her emotional connection to us, so I believe she's still okay," Alexander asserts.

I can't help but feel confused right now; it's been 30 plus years since Caspian's interacted with us as a family, and here he is working with us as if he never left. How did he even know about Danika? I guess my suspicions were right and he has been keeping track of us. I wonder how he felt about us bringing her into the family, and does he know Elijah gave her his ring to use?

"So, what is the plan now?" I ask.

"I think we should just wait and see what happens. I've been hanging around here lately and gathering some information about the Cerberus. Let's just see how it pans out."

I nod, and then realize that maybe Constance saw this coming…maybe she knew Caspian was around.

"Sophia, you do realize Alex has your thoughts still connected right?" Constance questions.

"Oh…um…yeah, sorry. I'm just a little overwhelmed right now."

"Don't you think we all are? But we're here to save Danika…we can figure everything else out later. Oh, and for your information, no I didn't see Caspian. Everyone knows I've been trying to, but we've been removed from him for too long – my connection to him was lost years ago. I would've prepared you all for this had I known."

"Will you two stop fighting? This is entirely my fault…I'm the one that left way back when, and I'm the one that decided to help Danika after I realized what was going on. I promise to explain everything later."

Elijah agrees. "Caspian's right. We're all in shock here; we're dealing with more emotions than we've had in a long time. Let's just focus on the task at hand and Caspian can join us back at the house later to discuss…"

Before he can even finish, the music stops, and every light goes out, only to have a large spotlight shine right in the middle of the stage, where Drake and Cyrus are now standing.

Cyrus begins to greet the patron's. "Thank you all for coming and showing your growing support for our way of life, and for our freedom from the vampire laws. These laws created by my siblings have held us back, prevented us from our rightful place as rulers of the Earth. Today is initiation and this brings us one step closer to taking back our rights. All of you who would like to pledge yourself to the fight, please step forward and bring your minion along if you have one. If you did not bring one and would like to pledge, we can provide one for you."

The crowd erupts in cheers and nearly two dozen vampires step forward, many with a mortal in tow. Caspian begins to step forward, but I grab his arm. "What the hell are you doing?"

"I need to appear as if I'm willing…someone needs to be on the inside to protect Danika and the family."

"And who will protect you?" I begin to panic at the thought of losing him again.

"Caspian, Sophia's right…this isn't the way." Elijah tries to stop him.

"Sorry, but I've been setting this up for a while now and I can handle it; you just have to trust me. I need to be on the inside, that's how we'll stop them."

Elijah releases Caspian's arm, nods, and peels my fingers from him, allowing him to join the others at the front of the stage.

Cyrus raises the mic to his mouth again. "As you know I am ready to pass on my family legacy and step down from the throne, from being the leader of the Cerberus, the true believers. Tonight, Drake is finally ready to accept his right as your leader. My son has presented to me a young woman, a young vampire, and he is ready to make her his queen. She is here and will lead you through the initiation tonight, and help Drake lead you to freedom for our kind!"

Again, the crowd cheers and excitement erupts through the masses. Drake takes the mic and holds his hand up to silence the crowd. "I would like to introduce you all to Danika." A woman with long black hair and a look that could freeze a person on their spot walks out with Danika on her arm. Danika is wearing a long white dress, with heavy makeup on and her short bob cut is pinned up with only little wisps falling down around her cherub-like face. I finally realize that Danika is nothing more than an innocent little girl. Someone did this to her and now because of the way I have acted, she's turned to these evil monsters. Drake reaches his hand out to her; she's reluctant to take it until the dark-haired woman leans over and whispers something in her ear. She takes Drake's hand and I can feel the waves of disgust coming off of her as he kisses her. "Danika, these are your people now; they are here for you, for us and for themselves. I promise your eternal life will be more fulfilling than you ever imagined."

With one swift raise of his arm the music starts again, the bass pumping so loud I swear the building's shaking. A small hiss is heard above the music and everyone looks up. I can't help but wonder what's happening, and thanks to still being connected through Alexander I can tell the rest of the family is wondering the same. The smell of blood then overpowers, and I feel the change happening, my jaw aches as I feel my fangs emerging and my eyes burning. I look up, the sprinklers begin to spin and blood pours from them over the crowd. More cheers break out as the patrons, dance and drink what they can catch. I look up at Danika and see the terror in her eyes; she's covered in blood and Drake proceeds to lick it off her. I notice her giving

Caspian a pleading 'help me look', and he notices too. Through our telepathic connection, we can form a plan.

"As soon as I get a chance I'm going to grab her. I'll run straight from stage left all the way by the wall to the stairwell. Try to block a path for me; when I grab her there will be a mad rush for me and I need your help to get her out. Someone's going to have to take care of the doorman so we can get out," Caspian explains.

"I think maybe we should wait till the actual initiation begins; once those that stepped forward are feeding on their victim they won't be so easily distracted," Elijah suggests.

"Maybe you're right; we'll do it once they start feeding and before Danika starts. We can't let her sink her teeth into a mortal or it's all over; she'll belong to them," Caspian agrees.

Alexander and Isaac agree to control the stairwell and the doorman; Elijah takes the area near the front as that's where the crowd is the densest. Constance, Florence and I all spread out between Elijah and Alexander; I believe the path should be clear enough for when Caspian gets Danika. As we prepare for our escape, the sprinklers start to slow and the blood shower ceases. I think the initiations are about to start. I still can't believe stuff like this happens in our world today; I guess some things never change.

Chapter 19

Breaking Free

A group of people walk out to the stage as Drake takes to the mic again. "My darling Danika, you may have your choice from the beautiful and tasty mortals. Tonight is your night."

Danika looks around, giving Caspian another pleading look. The dark-haired vampire that led Danika to the stage whispers something to her again and Danika nods as she begins to inspect the available selection. I notice her eyes filling with tears as she tries to fight the urge to break down.

"I…I think this one will do." She takes a young woman by the hand.

"Now the rest of you may choose yours." Drake insists as he leads the remaining mortals to those at the front of the stage ready to pledge to the Cerberus.

I can't help but wonder if these mortals think they will be Embraced or if they have been compelled to obey. I wish we could help them, but Danika's our concern tonight.

"Once your new queen has pledged, you may join her and pledge your immortal life to us."

I look at Elijah for guidance, *"How's our plan going to work now?"*

Caspian responds, *"I must move now before it's too late. Are you all ready?"*

We all agree and brace for what's to come as soon as Caspian grabs, Danika. With one last nod from each of us, he catches Danika's attention and shakes his head to the side, encouraging her to step away from Drake and the rest of the vampires on stage. She takes the hint and slowly steps to the side. One swift move and Caspian jumps on the stage scoops Danika up and she wraps her arms around his neck. With her in his arms he leaps through the air, nearly flying 20 feet over the crowd and landing perfectly between us and the wall. He runs like Superman and reaches the stairs in a Nanosecond. As the crowd tries to rush him, we fight them off, also trying to close in on the stairwell for our escape.

"No, let them go. We will find them later," Drake commands.

We're able to escape to the stairwell and out the exit. Alexander telepathically directs Caspian to our car and he is already there when we arrive. Danika's protesting as she realizes we're involved in saving her.

"Danika, I'm so sorry that you felt like you had to leave," I plead as Caspian holds her from running.

"Really? You sure the hell could've fooled me when you were beating me to the ground."

"Okay, so I went a little overboard. I really am sorry. I should've handled the situation better. I know I haven't been easy on you, but you're my sister. I didn't want to let you in because it broke me when Caspian left, I swore I wouldn't let anyone hurt me like that again."

Caspian lowers his head, "Sophia, I'm sorry I hurt you, but please know I was never very far from you. I always knew what was happening with our family and swore to protect you all. I know I hurt you guys more than anyone before and I never wanted to see you hurt again. I guess I just never clued into how badly it hurt you."

Florence interrupts, "I love to see all my children having a heart to heart, but can we please go home for this? I don't think we should stay here like sitting ducks."

"Alex and I will go grab Ebony and Eliza and meet the rest of you at home," Matilda suggests.

We all agree, and Danika gets in the car with Florence and Elijah as I jump in Isaac's car with Constance and Caspian. Driving away, I can't take my eyes off Caspian, he's back; he's really back. Tonight so much is happening, but I can honestly say this is something I never expected. All of a sudden, I feel a vibration from my back pocket.

Pulling out my cell, I see that a text from Nathanial has just come through. *Any news yet? Matt and I are a little worried.*

I quickly type back, '*on our way home; we got her and OMG Caspian too.*' I hit send.

"Is that your boyfriend you're texting?" Caspian tries to break up some of the tension in the car.

"Yeah, Nathanial. He's fantastic and I think you two will get along great."

"I think you might be right; anyone that loves my baby sister the way I've witnessed him loving you is worthy of my approval."

I panic at his comment; what does he mean by the way he's seen Nathanial love me. He didn't…no, Caspian wouldn't have seen us make love, would he? "What do you mean?" I ask with slight caution.

"I've seen the way that boy looks at you, and the way you look at him. It reminds me of Ashley," Caspian admits.

"I'm sorry."

"I'm happy to have had the short amount of time I did with Ashley. I'm just sorry it was cut short by my lack of control. Just promise me you will be cautious…I'd never want you to experience the pain I did."

"I've learned from your misfortunes. I'm sorry that things turned out poorly for you and wish so badly that I could've fixed things back then. I won't let the same thing happen to me. Nate is fully aware of what we are. I love him so much and we are very honest with one another."

"I think that was my biggest mistake…I didn't trust Ashley with my heart if she found out the truth. I know better now; I only wish it wasn't too late."

Caspian and I go on talking just like old times; Isaac and Constance are quiet in the front seat and don't join in the conversation. They only sit there hand in hand as Isaac takes us home; takes Caspian home, where he belongs.

Chapter 20

Together Again

The moment we pull into the drive, Matt and Nathanial both come racing out of the house. Nathanial runs straight to me, with sheer panic across his face, "Oh my God you're hurt… what happened?"

"What are you talking about? I'm fine; you don't need to worry about me."

"Sophia, you're covered in blood…matter of fact you all are. Someone better tell me what the hell happened tonight. Where's everyone else?"

"Okay, calm down, they're on their way. Alex and Mati went back to the pub to pick up Ebony and Eliza. This blood is from the club; they turned sprinklers on that sprayed blood everywhere. No one got hurt, I promise."

"That's the most sadistic thing I've ever heard," Nathanial says with disgust.

"The entire scene was a little disturbing. You will not believe what it's like there."

"You can tell me all about it later." Then he whispers, "How are you handling all this?"

"I'm okay, don't worry about me. I'm just happy my family is back together again. My whole family is back together now; including Caspian."

"I'm so happy for you, sweetie, but are you sure he's gonna stay?"

"I don't know if anyone here will allow him to leave again," I admit.

"I can hear you two," Caspian jokes.

Smiling at the brother I missed so much, I say, "Good…then you're prepared. Caspian, I would like to formally introduce you to the man who pulled me out of my shell and showed me how to love again. This is Nate, and Nate, this is my brother Caspian."

With a clearing of his throat, Matt interrupts, "And I'm Matt, but I guess I don't matter much."

"Hi, Matt, great to meet you." Caspian holds out his hand, and Matt shakes it.

Elijah and Florence arrive with Danika just after us and lead us all back into the house. Just as we are stepping through the front door, Alexander pulls up with the girls. Matt waits for Ebony while the rest of us go in, and the moment Caspian walks into the family room he notices Ms. Edwina sitting in the chair to the right of the fireplace.

"Ms. Edwina, is it really you?" He bolts over and leans down to greet and hug her.

"I'm sorry; sorry I betrayed you and your mother. I let you all down."

"Now Caspian dear, accidents happen. Mother and I always knew that something could happen. What we were looking for were vampires who didn't plan to intentionally kill or harm mortals. It's been long enough… time for you to let go. You've shown more remorse than most mortals would. It's time to forgive yourself," the wise woman encourages.

"She's right Caspian; it's time for you to come home. Both you and Danika belong here with us," Florence says. Her demeanor is subtle…she appears almost defeated.

Taking turns, everyone takes showers to remove the dried blood from the club off us; one by one, we rejoin the rest of the family and our close friends. As the night goes on our family not only talks about what happened tonight but as any family would we talk about our problems? Caspian agrees to spend the night and continue our conversation in the morning.

"I'm really sorry, but I really just want to go to bed," Danika admits.

"I think we all should," Elijah agrees.

It's late, but Nathanial goes home, and Matt agrees to drive Ebony, her sister, and Grams home. They all agreed we needed to be alone as a family. Florence fixes up the guest room for Caspian. I guess we'll just discuss everything in the morning. I know I won't sleep much; I'm still in a state of shock that Caspian's back.

***

I hear a slight rap on the large oak door to my room. "Come in."

Caspian opens the door, "Hey I thought we could chat like old times. I just don't think I'll sleep well tonight."

"I was thinking the same thing," I say with a little giggle.

“Why don’t you tell me a little more about this Nate character.”

“Well first off, he’s not a character; he is amazing. Nate’s very supportive of our family and he comes from such a good family too. The funny thing is, we all feel like we can’t keep any secrets from him. For some reason, he just sucks secrets out, without even knowing it. Our friend Matt that was here too, he says it’s a special ability.”

“Okay, that’s interesting, but what about Matt? How does he even know all this?”

“Well, he is a descendant of a guardian, and he too will be one when he passes on.”

“What on earth is a guardian?”

“Oh, well they are like guardian angels for witches and other supernatural beings. A guardian helps to train them and protect them. They have supernatural powers and pretty much know everything. Guardians are chosen from birth and begin training right away. They don’t complete training until after they die. It’s really neat. Not the dying part, but the whole training and how much they know.”

“Sounds like it.”

Caspian and I spend hours just talking. I fill him in on everything that’s been going on; he admits to knowing a lot of what we as a family have been up too.

“Tell me more about what you have been doing,” I request.

“Not a lot really. I have just been making sure the family is doing okay. I was there the night Nate got attacked and almost showed myself then. I thought Alex was going to need my help, but Isaac came to the rescue. And during your big fight with the Cerberus, I kept a watchful eye. Even before all this, I was always close. A few times I disappeared for a bit, but always came back to be close to the family.”

"I knew I've spotted you nearby before. Now, why didn't you come home if you were so close?"

"Because I had already hurt you all so much, I didn't want to take a chance of making things worse."

"Caspian, what happened with Ashley was an accident. We all know that and never blamed you."

"I blame myself. I should've been honest with her like you are with Nate."

"I didn't want to tell him; there was just no hiding it anymore, he had proof," I admit.

"I can understand that, but it must be so much better with him knowing."

"It is, but I was pretty scared telling him."

"How did he take it?"

"Like he saw my eyes change; it wasn't even important to him. I can't wait for you to get to know him."

"Me too; I really hope to be around a little bit more again."

"What do you mean, 'hope you will be around a little bit more'? You're back, end of story," I say, with fear that he'll correct me.

"Sophia, this is all something to talk more about in the morning when the family is with us."

"Ouch, the brush off."

"Yup; so, you ready for bed yet? We have been chatting for a few hours now."

A few more minutes pass and Caspian returns to the guest room. I turn on my stereo, letting it play randomly as I lie back on my bed. What a night this has been. Danika running away has brought Caspian back to us. I have to remember to thank her in the morning.

Oh God, then I have to deal with this fantasy of her thinking she's in love with me. I really hope we can get past all this. Maybe it's time my sibling rivalry should get tossed in the trash. Danika handled herself so well tonight; I think the whole family has underestimated her strength. I get lost in my thoughts and drift off to sleep.

Chapter 21

Awakening the Savior

Morning comes soon and the family gathers around the large mahogany dining table. Florence brings out some warm blood coffee. I love this stuff, and it's the perfect combination of blood and espresso warmed to the perfect temperature. She's also prepared some blood sausage; with everything going on since New Year's I forgot how much I actually enjoy sitting around the table to eat like a family. As Matilda helps Florence serve the meal, I pull my legs up to my chest, resting the heels of my feet on the edge of my chair. The pink flannel pajamas I'm wearing are perfect to rest my head on, soft and warm. Lifting my head, I pull my coffee mug to my face as I raise my head, I take a deep breath and enjoy the wonderful aroma, the two distinct flavors of coffee and blood complimenting one another. With a habitual blow into the mug, I take a small sip, allowing the flavors to dance around in my mouth as they flow down to warm my throat, soothing the burning and ache of hunger inside of me. We all thank Florence for her wonderful meal; she's the perfect mother figure. Florence is one of the most caring women I've ever met. I know she never had children in her mortal life;

she said she wasn't able too. Being over three centuries old, Florence never knew the reasons for her infertility. I know she wanted children, so to have us around and considering us her children has been and still is a great pleasure for her. What she doesn't realize is that it's even better for us. I love seeing her like this right now, so happy and relaxed. Last night was a difficult night for her; almost losing Danika nearly destroyed her. I've never seen her so distraught before, between Danika and Caspian it was nearly too much for her to handle. Now today, a new kind of peace that we haven't seen in years shines across her ageless face.

"Thank you for the meal Florence, delectable as always," Elijah complements. "So, I believe we have some matters to discuss. Caspian and Danika, maybe we should start with Danika."

Danika sinks in her seat, preparing for the big lecture. "I'm sorry," she mutters.

"No Danika, I'm sorry. I shouldn't have always been so hard on you. I feel really terrible that I pushed you into the arms of the Cerberus." I release my tension and allow the sincerity to come through in my words.

"I had no clue they were Cerberus until they mentioned it last night. I'm so glad you all came to save me. It was awful there. Drake is not nice and tried to force himself on me; his dad actually saved me and made Drake stop. Then that awful woman that prepped me for the initiation. I just can't believe the things that happened last night and the things I saw. I thought my vulnerability was gone…I mean I'm a vampire. Yet they controlled me like a puppet. I was terrified! Cas…ah, I mean, Caspian…was the nicest to me. I feel so stupid for not clueing in that you were the long-lost brother I always hear about around here," she rants uncontrollably.

“I didn’t want you to know. I only started going to Club VC because I saw Drake trying to lure you. I had to protect my family and you’re part of that family, even if we hadn’t met before the club. I’ve seen you through so much, and I feel like I know you very well Danika. You’re far too trusting and need to learn a lot. After all, you’re only sixteen, less than two years as a vampire. You would still be a teenager if you were mortal, and we all need to realize you are still a teenager. Now, don’t think I mean that in a bad way. All I mean is that you need to gain some life experience and enjoy being a teen for now since you’re stuck as one forever. You are a smart girl, I see that. Just know not everyone makes a good friend.”

“I know, but can we stop with the lecture?” she pouts.

Elijah reaches for Danika’s hand. “I don’t think he means to lecture you, none of us do. We just want you to understand that we care and want to help you.”

“I know, I just...I just acted so childish. I’m sorry.”

“I think that we all need to learn that even though we are immortal, we’re still a family, and with a family comes certain problems and disagreements. Siblings fight, parents and children disagree and with blended families like ours comes adjustment periods. In your case Danika, you still need to adjust to the loss of your old life, your mortal life,” Florence encourages.

Constance adds, “I still keep an eye open for information on your mortal family; they’re still looking for you. It’s been less than two years and they’ve not forgotten about you, so how can we expect you to forget about them.”

Danika sits in silence as the tears stream down her face. I decide to share my new revelation. “I never realized how hard this must be for you. When I was Embraced, I still had my brother, and he was the only family that mattered to me. Mati was alone and prepared to die; this was a second chance at life for her. Danika, you had no choice, when you were attacked in the streets of a tourist town."

"What exactly is your story, Danika?" Caspian inquires.

"Well about two years ago, when I was fifteen, by the way, you all know my birthday is coming up, right?" She winks and continues, "I ran away from home. My mom and I got in a fight…I always felt compared to my older brother. He was the light in my parent's eyes, where I could never do anything right. I guess some things never change," she smirks. "Well, I was only gone for about two hours, just walking around the streets of Banff, Alberta…that's where I grew up. I was just out back of the hospital when I was attacked. I never saw his face, but I knew it was a man. I could feel the scruff of his facial hair rub against my neck when he bit me. That was the last thing I remember, at least until I woke up at the Pierce's home. They explained that Constance found me in the street. She noticed the bite mark on my neck and blood stains on my mouth. She felt it was best to bring me home and help me through the Embrace, although she admitted to me she hoped she was wrong and that I would just heal. Of course, there was no such luck and the Embrace began shortly after. The vampire that Embraced me just left me there to die, or to wreak havoc on the town. The Pierce family took me in and showed me how to survive; they kept me well hidden, as posters were coming up until last summer when we moved."

"Knowing this family the way I do, I assume they disguised you and Elijah was able to take care of an identity change and documentation," Caspian confirms.

"You do know us well," Elijah laughs.

“How ‘bout you Caspian; what have you been up too since you left?” Danika asks and the rest of us listen intently.

“Well, I never really left. I’ve always followed the family wherever you’ve gone. I did a little vacationing, but for the most part, I stayed close and just threw out things to make it appear like I was elsewhere.”

“I should kick your ass for putting us through all this. If you were watching us the whole time, didn’t you see what your leaving did to our family, to Sophia?” Alexander explodes in a fury.

“Yeah, I did, but I always believed you were better off without me around, even if it hurt you.”

“So, what’s your plan now; I assume you’re staying?” Constance adds.

“Ummm, well I have other plans.”

“Are you kidding? You’re gonna leave again?” Alexander pounds his fist on the table, rattling everything on it.

“Not really leaving. I need to join the Cerberus; they’re going to be after you and me both now. I plan to beg for forgiveness and initiate. This way I can find out what their plans are and try to foil them.”

Elijah shakes his head as he reaches for Florence’s hand. “I don’t know about this plan. We can handle them, and with you, on our side, we’ll be even stronger. You could get yourself destroyed. The moment you resurface to them, they’ll gut you.”

“I’ve survived on my own for centuries. I was nearly 200 years old when I joined your family…I think I can manage. I promise to keep in contact; I’ll let the dust settle for a bit before I go back. I’ll stay here when I’m in Wenham and not Boston.”

“It’s your choice, but I think I speak for all of us when I say I do not like this idea,” Elijah concedes.

“Can I come? I’m the one they want, let me help.” Danika jumps at the chance to be involved.

“Absolutely not!” Everyone in the room shouts at once.

Danika sinks back in her chair, looking defeated again. I think we need to work on our relationship as sisters, even as a family. My feelings for Danika change from spite to concern; I want to protect her now that I saw her vulnerability last night.

Chapter 22

Ebony's Magical Tests

"Hey Eliza, can you grab me some dragon's blood?" I scream to my sister as I prepare a potion in the kitchen.

"Yup, be right there," Eliza replies.

Grams sits just off in the corner of the kitchen, shaking her head. I know she's wondering why Eliza and I always have to holler back and forth to each other. The fact is I'm just learning how to make these potions, and I really don't want to leave it alone. Kinda like home economics class, they always say never leave anything cooking unattended.

Eliza comes back in the kitchen and passes me the dragon's blood. "What exactly are you making?"

"Just a courage potion…I want to have a good supply. You never know when we may need it."

"Okay, fair enough. While you're at it, why not make one to increase our magical powers? That might come in handy as we begin our search for the demon that killed mom and dad."

Together Eliza and I make up various potions and place them in the large apothecary cabinet in our kitchen. Grams has been working very hard with us, training us to fight the evil that will undoubtedly arrive for us soon. The stronger our powers become the easier we are to find, and we must be prepared. The fight with the Cerberus only proved that we can't do this on our own yet.

"Hey Eb, have you talked to Dakota since the fight?"

"We texted a few times; he has a girlfriend now, so he's a little preoccupied," she laughs.

It has been over a month since the big fight and since the rescue mission to save Danika. Maybe we should gather everyone, just to make sure there are still no plans for Drake or Cyrus to come after the Pierces. It's still hard to imagine that Caspian was able to talk Drake into giving him a second chance after helping Danika escape. I know Sophia is having a hard time with Caspian when he's in the Boston area; she worries so much. I wonder if he'll be rejoining them soon.

As I place the last bottle in the apothecary, my phone vibrates in my back pocket. Eliza catches the vial that slips from my grasp at the surprise butt massage. Grams just chuckles and shakes her head again. Looking at the caller ID I see Matt's number and race up to my room for some privacy.

∞ ∞ ∞

"Hi Hun, when are you coming to get me?"

"Will an hour be enough time for you?" Matt asks, his smile showing through his voice.

"Yeah, that's great. We still going for lunch with your mom and dad?"

“That’s the plan; I wish I could just have a normal party with my friends for my birthday.”

I listen to him complain for a while, and when he’s done I run back downstairs. “Eliza are you sure you can handle everything for Matt’s surprise party?”

“Ah, I don’t know. I’ve never been to a party before,” she answers with a little glare. “I think I can handle things…Sophia, Mati, and Danika will be here shortly to help me; just clean up this potion mess before you leave.”

This should be so much fun, and Matt doesn’t suspect a thing. We’re not planning a big party, just those closest to us…my family, his and the Pierce’s. I wonder if Caspian will come to the party; I guess I’ll just have to wait and see. In the meantime, I need to clean up and get ready for lunch with Matt and his family.

∞ ∞ ∞

With our lunch date, a success Matt’s parents suggest a hike as a means of distracting him. “I just have to go home and change my shoes,” I bait.

“That’s fine, why don’t we just follow you and Matt, and we can go from there,” suggests his mom.

Before long we’re back at the manor…it looks as if the others have hidden their cars successfully. I suggest Matt comes in and introduce his parents to my Grams, something of an excuse to get everybody in the house. Opening the door, I notice things seem out of place, even for a party. Then a large crashing sound comes from Gram’s office. Matt and I both run to the sound; my heart pounds faster and faster with the fear of losing Gram’s. Down the hall, I throw open the door and see Gram's and Eliza using magic as the Pierce family physically fight a being, not of this world. He looks human, just badly scarred and with yellow eyes; he looks evil. I dart to the opposite corner and join Gram's and Eliza, who is flipping frantically through the Book of Shadows.

"Got it," she says with hope and points to a chant to block a Pyro, which they seem to believe him to be, out of our realm and into the depths of the underworld.

The three of us begin to chant.

Lady and Lord of the day,
Protect us from this evil prey.
Banish him into the depths,
Allow him power, no more.
With the power of thee,
We banish he.
So mote it be,
So mote it be,
So mote it be.

The entity before us begins to shake and spin…our vampire friends back up; light beams through the office window and he bursts into millions of particles and disappears.

Quiet takes over for a brief moment; we all look around, ensuring everyone we care about is safe. "Oh my God, that was amazing. What just happened?" I rhetorically ask.

Grams hugs both Eliza and I. "Well, girls, I believe you just defeated your first demon."

Cheers erupt in the room, and Matt bolts towards me, his parents only a few steps behind, congratulating us and hugging us. Well, I guess if Matt's parents didn't know about me before, they sure do now. I take solace in the fact their family is very much aware of the supernatural. I'm just glad they never noticed anything out of sorts with the Pierce family. I would hate for their secret to come out because of me.

"Well, now we have two things to celebrate. Why don't we get things cleaned up around here and we can have a little party," Florence suggests?

"We'll go tidy up out there as you all discuss what happened. This will give you some privacy," Matt's dad suggests, not realizing that the Pierces have long since known about my family and our powers.

"Oh Matt, I'm so sorry. This was supposed to be a surprise party for you," I rest my head on his shoulder. "This ruined your party."

"Nothing's ruined, and I'm definitely surprised," he jokes. "Hey, everyone's here but Nate. Where is he?"

"Oh no!" Sophia shouts as she runs past me.

The rest of the Pierce family breaks into laughter.

"What did we miss?" Matt smiles with slight confusion.

"Sophia locked Nate into a safe room." Alexander bursts out laughing again. "He's not happy; she threw him over her shoulder and tossed him in there like a sack of potatoes." He chuckles some more.

Then we all hear the bickering, "You didn't have to do it like that," Nathanial huffs.

"Sorry, I didn't want you to get hurt," Sophia defends.

"Oh, but a bruised ego caused by my petite girlfriend shoving me around's okay?"

"Okay, maybe I went a little overboard; I'm sorry."

"Just ask next time...I would've gone in on my own accord."

A moment later they walk back into the office hand in hand.

"Hey, Matt, happy birthday. Did you see any of the action?" Nathanial glances in our direction.

"Not really, got her here just in time for Ebony to help do a magnificent spell." He chuckles at his corny play on words. "Now, there was supposed to be a party…let's go celebrate me!"

Chapter 23

Back to Normal

So much has happened in the past few months. I'm excited to finish out the rest of the school year. As we pull into the parking lot at school, I notice Nathanial pulling up right behind us. I wait for him as the rest of my family goes inside.

"Hi, sweetie." He greets me with a small soft kiss.

"Hi, how's your mom and dad doing? I feel like it has been forever since I've seen them."

"Good, I had a little talk with them last night."

"About what?"

"I took Florence's advice and decided to see if they would still like to have another child."

"That's great, I'd hate to heal her womb and then find out they don't want another child."

"Well, I think you can start anytime. Mom and Dad said they feel so blessed to have Luke and me but still would love to have another. Mom says they've been looking at adoption."

"Really? Well, maybe I can help with that. They aren't happy that you will be at college in the next few years?"

"They said they feel too young for an empty nest. So many of their friends waited to have children and their kids are all small still. I think they feel a little left out, not having small kids to go to birthday parties and such with."

"Well it's settled; maybe we can start today after school."

Nathanial and I make plans for me to visit his family later this afternoon and then head into class. It's going to be nice to not be preoccupied by danger. Although I am a little worried about Caspian's plan to go back to Club VC and ask for his second chance, he said today he will go back to Boston more permanently, for now at least. Until now he's only spoke to Cyrus and Drake on the phone, begging for forgiveness. Putting my concerns in the back of my mind I decide to continue on and enjoy the day. I chuckle at the thought that less than a year ago I was completely against coming back to high school, and now I look forward to it.

The day continues on in an uneventful manner, until fifth period I notice Nathanial's friend Ben down the hall from my locker. Walking towards him I hear a female voice attempting to speak softly, but of course, I can hear every word. I recognize the voice; it's that awful girl Mel that's so mean to Ebony. Today her victim is Ben. Ben notices me approaching and waves me off, but in my usual non-compliant way, I keep walking towards them.

"What's your problem today, Mel?" I snarl.

"Well, now it's you. How dare you just butt in like this? This has nothing to do with you."

"You know something, Mel, some of us are tired of you believing that you run the school. Being head cheerleader means nothing to anyone but you. So how about I give you a piece of advice?"

“Oh, really…you’re going to give me advice? How about I give you some…mind your own business or else.”

“Ladies cut it out. Sophia, just go to class, I can handle this.” Ben interrupts.

“Shut up, loser,” Mel glares at Ben.

Placing my hand on her shoulder I say, “Hey, why don’t you tell me a little more about this little threat you’re so keen on making.”

She pushes my hand away, “Are you stupid? I know you’re new here, but I can destroy you. Dating the most popular guy in school doesn’t make you special. Now take a hike.”

“You have no idea who you’re talking to, you smart ass little...”

“Sophia.” Alexander shouts, “What the heck are you doing?”

“Just getting ready to take some trash out,” I smirk in Mel’s direction and Ben bursts out in laughter.

“Oh, you didn’t...”

Ben grabs her and pulls her in the opposite direction as Alexander holds me back. I’ve had enough of this chick, thinking she’s the queen bee and that she can treat everyone like crap. A teacher pokes his head out of class and instructs us to return to our classes. I guess I’ll have to deal with her later, and then I can ask Ben what the problem was. We all go our separate ways and I try to calm myself during final period.

∞ ∞ ∞

After school, Nathanial and I go back to his house as planned. I’ll begin trying to restore the damage done to Mrs. McCord the night of Nathanial’s birth. The McCord’s aren’t home from work yet, so

Nathanial and I decide to clean the house and start supper. I want his mom to relax tonight after I do my first healing session. I offer to prepare the meal as Nathanial vacuums. In the fridge, there's a whole chicken in a plastic Ziploc bag thawing on a plate. I look around the kitchen for a roasting pan and spices. It only takes a few minutes and I have the chicken prepped, along with veggies and potatoes all in the pan; with the oven preheated I place dinner in and set the timer.

By the time Nathanial's parents arrive home from work, dinners finished, and I have the table set. Mrs. McCord seems surprised at mine and Nathanial's efforts, "Oh kids, it smells so wonderful, and everything is so clean! I can't tell you how much I needed this today. I'm exhausted and had a very trying day at work. Thank you so much."

"Mom, you do so much for our family, Sophia and I thought you could use a night off."

"I have the best kids in the world, and they pick the best girlfriends too."

Nathanial leans down and hugs his mom as she sits at the dinner table. I walk up behind her chair and wrap my arms around her, placing my hands lightly on her abdomen. She places her hands over top of mine, which helps add to the energy. When she gives a small wiggle in her chair, I pull back.

"Sorry Sophia, I think I'm in need of that chicken you made. My stomach feels a little funny."

Nathanial and I both look at one another, "No worries, I am just feeling huggy today. Let me serve you."

"No need to serve us, please just sit and enjoy the meal with us."

We enjoy the meal Nathanial and I prepared together as well as normal dinner conversation. Mr. and Mrs. McCord tell us about their days at work and as soon as dinner is finished Mrs. McCord excuses herself to call it an early night. Nathanial and I take care of the dishes and leftovers. We both know her stomach issue and unexpected fatigue is from the healing process…I just never expected it to begin so soon. My only thought is that because of my strong emotional ties to this family, more of my energy goes into the healing. I'll continue trying to heal her whenever I get a chance. I don't want to make it too obvious; if I do it every time I see her they may put two and two together.

∞ ∞ ∞

After Nathanial drops me off at home I check with the others to see if anyone's heard from Caspian; no one has. I just go to my room; I'm worried about him, about what Drake and Cyrus will do to him. I hear a soft knock at my door and then it creeps open. Danika walks in and sits next to me on my bed.

"Sophia, so much has happened, I really think it's time we just hash things out. I want to get this out of the way and be sisters."

"I think that is the most mature thing you've ever said Danika and a great idea. I'm really sorry for how hard I was on you; I never really gave you a chance and just assumed you'd screw up."

"Well, I guess you were right…I did mess up pretty bad. I should've talked to someone about Drake when he started pressuring me to come out with him. I probably should have talked to you about my jealousy of you and Nate started becoming a real issue. I didn't mean to hurt you when I kissed him; I just had to know what I was feeling."

"You know I overreacted…I should have never come after you like that. It's just, everyone knows that Nate and I are soul mates and to have...well it's all over now, so just promise no more flirting with my guy."

"I think we both know that won't happen anymore. I just felt…I just…well, at least I know a little about myself now. I just don't see finding anyone for me here. Small towns like this can't have many like me."

"Like you? Danika, first off, I don't think anyone is like you, but not the way you think. If you are talking about being gay, that doesn't make you an outcast. Honestly, it shouldn't even make you different; who you like or fall in love with is not a choice. So, you're gay, big deal. You are still my bratty little sister and I still care about you. One day you will find someone to love and they will love you in return. Now, I don't ever want to hear another derogatory comment about yourself or your sexuality, do you understand me?"

"Okay, calm down Sophia, I don't want you to get all worked up again. I already know where that gets me." She jokes.

We stay up most of the night talking and dealing with our issues. I realize that I'm so hard on her because I care, and she realizes that she isn't actually in love with me, but at least she understands a little more about herself now. I think we can get past most of the tension between us. Neither of us will pretend that things are perfect, but we're getting there.

Chapter 24

Caspian's Punishment

Returning to Club VC and offering myself is all I can do to try and save my family. After 30 years I finally have them back in my life, and I won't allow anything to hurt them the way I did when I killed Ashley. Saving Danika from initiation was only the beginning, but I expect to be punished for my actions. Walking in, I hold my head up high knowing that Cyrus and Drake have already been notified of my arrival, courtesy of the guard at the door.

"Cas, we didn't expect to see you back here, even after we spoke, I didn't think you'd have the guts to show," Drake announces as I walk into the main club.

"I came to plead for forgiveness for my actions early this year."

"Please, refresh our memory, as there are so many initiates that defy us," he says with utter sarcasm.

"I beg for my king's forgiveness for taking your queen initiate," I say with a bow on one knee, being extremely formal with all my jesters. I must play this perfectly.

“You admit to stealing my future queen; how would you like to explain this deviant action against all of us?”

“Cyrus, Drake please forgive me. Danika and I have become friends and nothing more. I felt protective of her and she pleaded with me to help her as she looked upon me. Her eyes were filled with pain and fear; I felt I was helping her. I haven’t seen her since that night. Since then I have searched in hopes to build her up and prepare her for her rightful place by your side, but to no avail.”

“You need to atone for your sins against us,” Cyrus insists with a strong gaze that I feel right through to my core.

“Of course, your majesty.” I agree, but it’s making me ill inside giving these two respect I don’t feel they deserve.

I sense others closing in on me. With a quick look over my shoulder, I see the goons that work for Cyrus and Drake. They grab me from behind; I know fighting won’t help my case, so I go willing with the brutes. The smirks on the leader’s faces send chills down my spine and leave me wondering what they have in store for me. The evil in the room is palpable.

I’m lead to the back of the club, down the same hallway that Drake took Danika the night of initiation (or at least the entrance that I last saw her enter). There’s several closed doors; the hallway is lit only by red lights. I’m led to the very last door at the end of the hall. Cyrus opens the door with a key that hangs around his neck on a gold chain and pushes me through the door. I stumble and fall down several stairs. The two goons and their leaders step down after me. One of the men picks me up and leads me to the back of the room. My extraordinary vision helps me to adjust to the dark. The room I’m pushed into is what seems to be an empty concrete cell; I can smell the mold around me. The cool damp room gives me an uneasy feeling.

"On your knees, son," Cyrus demands, and the man holding me pushes me to the ground. Each one of the brutes grabs one of my arms, nearly ripping them from the sockets. I hear a rattling behind me. Cyrus stands in front of me while Drake moves behind me.

"You dishonored us and now you must pay. You came here to ask forgiveness and to be allowed back into our clan, our family. Well, for the next thirty days you will prove your worthiness to us," Cyrus nods.

I feel Drake at my wrist; he shackles me with heavy chains. One wrist at a time, then the ankles; one final large chain gets wrapped around my waist, crossing in the front, over each shoulder and crossing again to wrap once more around my waist. I look over my shoulder to see Drake lock everything to the concrete wall. These chains are heavy, even for me. I'm sure it's to guarantee I can't escape.

"Now you may stand," Cyrus instructs, and I see his hand lifting to guide me.

Drake walks around to stand face to face with me. "The last time you were here you stole my queen from me, now it's my turn to take something in return."

"Yes, master."

A smile breaks across Drakes face; I know something is coming but...all of a sudden, I receive an uppercut right under the chin. My head flops back with such force I feel a vertebra snap and my entire body slumps as paralysis takes over; only the chains hold me inches from the ground. Drake continues to beat my limp body…blood pours momentarily from my mouth and nose along with the cuts from the beating, but my increased healing is helping to slow the blood and heal the cuts. I know it will take a few hours at least to repair the damage done to my spinal cord, allowing me no defense mechanism.

Once pleased with the damage done and pain I'm suffering Drake stops.

"This is just the beginning, Cas…you will pay for taking Danika from me, from all of us. She would have been a great queen. Your punishment will happen at least twice a day for the next month, maybe even more if I feel the need. I will allow others who have offered their eternity to our cause to punish you as well, at my discretion of course. If I feel you need blood to survive you will receive it, but you will not be fed just to satisfy hunger. Do you understand the terms of your punishment?"

I roll my eyes up and down as if nodding. Then blackness begins to take over as I lose consciousness from the injuries, pain and blood loss.

Chapter 25

Panic

It's been nearly three weeks since Caspian returned to the Cerberus at Club VC and we haven't heard a word from him. Constance insists he hasn't been destroyed yet. Her visions aren't giving her much information, but she's seen him come back around. I guess that's good news. I only hope he's doing okay and that they aren't brainwashing him or something…we just got him back, I can't lose him again. Since none of us can return to the club and look for information, we're just going to have to wait until Caspian contacts us or comes home.

"Earth to Sophia… hey, are you okay?" Ebony nudges me.

"Yeah sorry, just thinking."

"Well, I just thought I'd let you know that you're up next for your Spanish oral presentation."

"Thanks. I guess I should pay a little attention." I give her a half smile, which makes me think of Nathanial. I shake off the thought and try to concentrate on the class.

The entire day drags on; I'm glad that school will be over soon. I guess I'm more of a teenager than I thought. When the day's over I meet with the rest of the gang, my family, Ebony, Matt and of course Nathanial…Ben joins us as well. Hanging around outside in the courtyard just chatting and minding our own business we notice that awful excuse for a girl Mel. Once again, she is picking on some poor soul.

Ben stands up from the bench he's been sitting on. "I'm so sick of this chick thinking she runs things around here. Someone needs to put a stop to her bullying."

"Dude, didn't you date her for a bit last year?" Nathanial chuckles.

"Oh, bite me; it was a moment of weakness," he storms over and gives Mel a piece of his mind. She turns her attack on him.

"I think she's getting worse," Ebony notes.

"I didn't think she could get any worse," Nathanial jokes.

We all watch as Mel and Ben go a few rounds back and forth. Ben turns and smiles at us then looks directly at Mel. "Have you ever noticed that the people that supposedly like you are only your friends because they're scared of you? You aren't the queen bee of the school, you're the queen bitch. I have one last suggestion for you; shut that filthy mouth of yours, mind your own business, and leave the rest of us alone."

Mel's jaw drops; no one's ever had balls enough to confront her and call her out. Ebony was the closest one to ever stand up to her. Everyone remaining in the courtyard cheers and high fives Ben as he walks away leaving Mel standing there in shock. Ben's grin reaches straight across his face as he returns to our group. He and Nathanial jump in the air and chest bump one another. "That was so cool, dude. What on earth possessed you to stand up to her?" Nathanial continues to congratulate Ben.

“I just can’t handle all the negativity coming from her. She prides herself on tearing others down…she’s evil spirited.”

“Wow Ben, you’ve always been a nice guy, but I’ve never seen you so passionate about something before. What’s got you on this savior kick?” Matt questions.

Ben chuckles, “I don’t know…just recently, I have this overwhelming urge to make things right. To help others.”

“I can understand that feeling. I felt the same before...” Ebony stops herself before saying too much to Ben. “Ah, before when, she attacked me and my family,” she nervously tries to cover.

After a while, Ben takes off and goes home, and the rest of us decide to go to Ebony’s. She’s agreed to help us find information on Caspian. We also want to look into what’s giving Ben this overwhelming feeling of goodness. There’s gotta be an explanation for it… people don’t just become do-gooders – or do they?

∞ ∞ ∞

Back at the manor, Eliza looks at the Book of Shadows to see if there’s anything that might explain why Ben’s niceness is exaggerated and why he’s got what we’ve nicknamed Robin Hood syndrome. In the meantime, Ebony uses tarot cards to try to get some answers about Caspian. She lays out a black velvet cloth on the table and begins to shuffle the deck of cards.

“I’m going to use the simplest layout three card spread. This shows us the recent past, the present, and the future. All I have to do is focus on him and what I want to know.”

“Well, let’s find out about his safety,” I suggest.

“That’s my thought exactly,” Ebony agrees and closes her eyes to focus as she shuffles the deck, once, twice, three times. Then she splits the deck in half and turns one-half of the deck 180 degrees, and shuffles three more times before placing the three cards out in front of her. “Okay, some cards look scary, but they need to be read in context, so before you freak out allow me to read and explain them to you. I promise to be honest no matter what I see. Are you ready for me to begin?”

“We understand. Go ahead and start the reading,” Alexander encourages.

Ebony nods and turns the first card; it says ‘judgment’ and is a picture of an angel blowing a horn, with seven notes coming from it, as the angel looks down on a man, woman, and child. It is reversed and facing those of us across the table from Ebony. She then turns the second card, placing it just to the right of the judgment card. This one is called the tower with a picture of exactly that, a tower, being struck by lightning and surrounded by darkness; flames pour from the windows of the tower as people dive to their certain death. This card faces Ebony. She’s slow to turn the final card, placing it on the far right. The final card is the six of wands; it’s a picture of young man riding a white horse with a crowd cheering him on. My mind is going crazy thinking what all these names and symbols might mean.

“So here, the first card is Caspian’s recent past…now for a vampire the timelines may be slightly different than with mortals, so I want you to just refer to this as his past. I won’t try to assume how far in the past…maybe we’ll figure it out with the reading. The same goes for the next two cards, the middle card is his present and the final card his future. Do you follow me so far?”

“Yeah go ahead, we get it,” Danika chews her lip with anxiety.

"Okay, Caspian's past is represented by a reversed judgment card. This suggests he is indulging in self-doubt, causing him to miss out on the brighter things life has to offer him. This card tells me he's not allowing himself to learn from his past mistakes and that he is overly hard on himself. Knowing Caspian's story, I assume this card has to do with Ashley and his self-chastising. He needs to forgive himself so that he can move forward." She looks around to all of us that are intently listening to her and nodding in agreement. Then she continues, "The second card is his present. The tower card suggests that he is feeling afraid, shaken and insecure. He's going through a major issue and it's causing him great amounts of pain, both physical and emotional. His world is being rocked and turned upside down right now. Caspian is suffering; I have to assume the Cerberus is making him pay for his betrayal. Now I know this may worry you but let me explain this final card, his future. The six of wands represents balance and victory. This tells me he will be successful, and the outcome is far greater than he ever imagined. A struggle has been overcome and others will want to celebrate in his victory. I see this card as meaning he comes through whatever he's facing now in the present and might even mean he's able to bring down the Cerberus. Good things are going to happen for Caspian, and he will start a new life, with a fresher and more positive outlook."

I start to crack a smile and Nathanial squeezes me. "This is good then, he'll be okay," I confirm.

"Yes, I believe he will, we just need to be patient," Ebony says with excitement.

Eliza walks over. "Ebony I'm so proud of you. You're really getting good at doing readings."

“Thanks, I’ve been working hard. I study the meanings almost nightly and do a self-reading every week or two.”

“Well, it seems to be paying off.”

Matilda interrupts, “How about you Eliza, did you have any luck with the book and Ben?”

“Not really; I mean I found some interesting stuff, but not anything that I think pertains to Ben. I have a feeling he’s just maturing and, like most people, are sick of rude, obnoxious little girls that think the world owes them.”

“Amen to that; guess God’s sent us an angel,” Matt jokes.

“That’s possible, but why does everything have to be male orientated? Maybe it was a goddess that sent him to us,” Eliza jokes back.

We all laugh, knowing that the Triggs family believes in various deities, both god and goddess. Their Wiccan way is really growing on me, so full of life and positivity. They use the natural energy around us to perform their magic. Maybe it’s time for Ebony to teach me a little more about her lifestyle and heritage, now that she’s a little more accustomed to it herself.

Chapter 26

Help

It's been a few months since Danika escaped the Cerberus and becoming their queen as they called it. I'm quite surprised that we haven't had any sightings of them. Talking with the family, we decide to call in the shapeshifters. They can help us scout the area to see if the Cerberus has members watching us or Danika again. They know where we go to school, and we know that the older members are self-made day walkers. I remember seeing Drake talking to Danika, shortly after we moved here. So, if he has been stalking her from the start, why would he just stop? Our allies should be here shortly, and we can see if they know anything.

In the meantime, Florence and Constance prepare us a wonderful meal; blood and basil soup and a blood tea infused with mint with plasma cake for dessert. Florence has been attempting different recipes with blood products instead of just whole blood. It's been good; the blood products still boost our energy and keep us fed, they just doesn't last as long as whole blood. This is good in the fact that we can survive as long as we get the various parts of the blood. Isaac brings home different types of blood and blood products. He's been working downstairs in a lab he built for the last little while. Isaac is trying to invent an organic blood, or manmade blood so to speak. He is hoping that if he can create blood for us, we will no longer need to feed from animals or the blood bank. He's attempting to use expired blood and blood products but hasn't been able to get it perfected enough for us to test. If successful, this may be a great discovery for him as a doctor too. To have the blood or parts of blood needed at all times, able to stock this created blood in the hospitals and blood banks could potentially save lives. There would be less concern with transmitting diseases and there would never be a shortage. I commend him for his efforts; I'd love to do more than meaningless jobs and school. After dinner, everyone just lounges around waiting for the Williams family to arrive.

Danika joins me in the art room. I think it will be nice to do a painting of her for the family.

"Why don't you sit in the lounge chair by the window?"

Danika takes a seat in the large classic looking chair. I grab my pencil to lightly sketch her outline, but something's wrong…she looks too stiff, too formal. "Danika, try to relax. Just be yourself."

"How do you suggest I do that?"

"Well first off, is that how you normally sit in that chair?"

"No, I usually sit here when I read."

"Okay, so grab a book and just read like you normally do."

She reaches to the side table and swings her legs over the arm of the chair. I begin by sketching the chair. First the oak legs round and stretching into a point, I do a rough outline of the chair, but then focus on the remaining wood detail; the end of the arms and the top of the chair with the extensive carving detail. Then I add a light sketch of Danika's body before I finish the chair with the red padded covering.

Danika's legs dangle off the one arm and her ankles are crossed, her upper body shifted so that her back rests on the opposite corner of the chair. I draw her as she sits and reads, one arm resting on the arm of the chair with the book in hand. She really is turning out to be a sweet girl now that I'm giving her half a chance. We still have issues, but what sisters don't? At least now I can call her my sister. As I finish the rough sketch I pull out my pastels and start working on filling in and bring the portrait to life. She's an easy model to draw, with only the slightest movements as she turns the book's pages. The entire piece doesn't take me long at all and right as I finish the doorbell rings. I cover my work to present later, but for now, I want to see Dakota and his dad.

∞ ∞ ∞

Danika and I both race out to the entrance. "Dakota," I yelp as I run to our friend and hug him. "Why'd you stay away for so long?"

"Just busy with school and all, how are things? Is Ebony here?"

I try not to chuckle, knowing he has it bad for Ebony, even though he's been dating. "No, her and Eliza are busy studying. They've been getting demon attacks recently and need to start preparing."

"Yeah, she mentioned something about that in an e-mail; pretty scary if you ask me."

Elijah walks to the entrance. "Girls, why don't you invite our guests in, rather than making them stand in the entryway."

"Oh…sorry. Please come have a seat. Can I get you a soda or something?" Danika offers as the other family members join us.

"Thank you, I'd love just water if you don't mind," Tamo requests.

Danika excuses herself to the kitchen and returns only moments later with beverages and cookies for our guests.

Elijah decides its best just to get down to business and fills the shifters in on what's been happening in the past weeks, and even months, since the fight we had with the Cerberus. Elijah summarizes mine and Danika's fight, Danika running away to Club VC, finding Caspian and saving Danika, the demon attack at the Triggs manor, and finally, Caspian returning to Club VC as a spy. He briefly spoke to them when Danika was missing so they could keep an eye out for her, and then when we found her. Now he feels it's important to give Tamo and the Williams family the full story.

"It's been over three weeks and we still haven't heard from him; we're not only concerned for him but for Danika too. The Cerberus leaders wanted to make her their queen, and I don't believe that they'd just give up that easily and forget about her. We just want to alert you that there may be some more action and check to see if you've noticed anything out of the ordinary."

"Elijah, we're so sorry your family has been through so much. I'll make sure our group keeps our eyes out for unusual behavior. I can't say that we've noticed anything, but we also believe the Cerberus was destroyed that night."

"We believed that we destroyed the ones in the New England area, but it appears they're a much larger group than we expected. I'm grateful for your continuing support; please know we're always here if you need anything."

Us teens realize we are not needed in the formal conversation and take Dakota out into the yard to toss the ball around. Alexander,

Matilda. Danika, Dakota and I are able to goof around. He can handle our strength and speed and hold his own against us. This makes a game of football a little more fun. Once the older members of our group finish discussing the matters at hand, Tamo calls for Dakota to go. "Son, we must get back and inform the tribe. You and the other boys can come hang out later."

Florence hugs our guests as they prepare to leave. "Thank you for coming, and please don't stay away for so long next time."

Once again everyone disburses, and I sneak off to the art room to put the finishing touches on my drawing of Danika. I think it's turning out great and will look wonderful on the walls with the rest of the family's portraits. I'll present it to the family later; for now, I think I'm going to go see what Nathanial is up too. Things have been a little crazy and I just miss relaxing with him. I gather my things and start to head to my car, thinking I'll surprise him and just show up at his house.

Pulling out of the garage I see Nathanial's silver car pulling up the long drive and can't help but giggle that he has the same idea as me. I re-park my car and run out to the front veranda to meet him.

"Hope I didn't interrupt any plans," he says as he gets out of his car.

"Only a surprise visit to my favorite guy."

"Really, do I have to go kick some poor guys butt for moving in on my gal?" He gives me his half smile and I run into his arms.

"You know that you're the only one for me, so how about you stop teasing me."

"Only if you ditch this guy and hang with me for the rest of the day."

I scowl at him and give him a light punch to the arm. "Fine, be that way. Why don't we go for a swim and then maybe we can go for a hike."

"That sounds great, but let's do the hike first. I am always lazy after swimming."

We start through the thick woods behind the house; the trees and wildflowers are all in full bloom now, and animals are scurrying on the ground as they search for food after the spring melt. Nathanial and I walk hand in hand down the small worn dirt path. We make our way up the mountain to the meadow, where families are enjoying the nice spring weather and a picnic. I show Nathanial how to track various animals and what the various footprints belong too.

"This is really interesting; thanks for sharing so much with me."

"Well, I figure since you're a part of my life you should know about what I do."

"I just love being up here with you. It's hard to believe I've never been to this meadow and seen the beauty up here before you came. I've grown up here my entire life, but whenever my family and I go camping or do outdoors stuff, we drive a little further into the mountains. We should bring my parents up here some time; I think they'd really enjoy it."

"Of course; speaking of your parents, how is your mom doing?"

"She's good; she still has no clue that whenever you are around her she gets the tired funny feeling. I even heard her tell dad it might be early menopause," he shivers his body at the thought of his mother's personal issues.

“I’m wondering if I can convince her that I’m learning Reiki and let me practice on her.”

“What the heck is Reiki?” Nathanial asks with a goofy look on his face.

With a good laugh, I explain, “Reiki is an ancient Japanese technique used for relaxation and stress relief. It also helps promote healing. It’s believed that by touching, one can move his or her life force energies into the other to help heal them. This is very true, although not everyone can perform it. When I heal someone, this is basically what I do, just on a much larger scale.”

“You know that might just work. We can tell mom you have been studying this and would like to see if it can help her to relax after work.”

“Maybe we should skip the swim and go to your house. Did your mom pick up another overtime shift this weekend?”

“No, but I know she’s been stressed about this whole lady business thing, and bills are getting tight now that dads slowed down at work. Not much construction work right now… everyone is taking it easy. I think they’re still concerned about another recession hitting as hard as the one a few years back”

We start back down towards the house. “Why didn’t you mention that your dad needed some work? I know my family would hire him and pay him very generously too.”

“I guess just a family pride thing. Sorry I didn’t tell you.”

We continue going over the options for his dad. I can discuss it later with Florence, Elijah, Constance, and Isaac. I know my family will hire him to work around the house and the offices; that’s what friends and family do for each other.

Chapter 27

Caspian's Torture

Drake and Cyrus have been torturing me since my return; I'm not even sure how long it's been, only that I'm so thirsty. I've heard that when a vampire starves they shrivel up and appear to die, but if they are given blood again they are resurrected. I believe this is what they are doing to me, and this is the most painful thing I've ever experienced. It feels as if every nerve ending in my body is on constant fire, like a firework spectacular going off within me. The shackles and even my clothes touching me are like razor blades or a million paper cuts. Feeling weaker by the moment and finding it difficult to keep my thoughts straight, I hear the door to the chamber open, and although I can no longer sense other supernatural beings I know they're here to beat me again. I believe my power of sensing others is depleted due to the starvation. As the footsteps draw closer they hammer into my head from the enhanced super hearing, probably magnified by the starvation as well. I try to block the sound but am too weak to control any of my original five senses. One of the bad traits of being a vampire; we must be healthy and well fed for the added benefits to work, yet normal human senses that are enhanced due to vampirism are harder to control when weak. The starvation has caused my rapid healing to cease, and due to the beatings, I've been receiving my eyes are almost completely swollen shut. I try to peer through the small opening left in my right eye and get a clue of who has come into the room, but no luck; everything is just a blur.

"Cas, you have now endured your 30 days of punishment, and I will now release you and allow you to feed." The voice I recognize as Drake announces as he approaches me to unlock the shackles.

The pain from his touch is nearly unbearable, but it only takes moments. Still difficult to see, I smell a mortal; my animalistic nature takes over and, like a police dog I sniff out the mortal in the room, pouncing and feeding. As the warm thick blood races down my throat, I feel my body beginning to heal and repair itself from her crimson life curing me almost as fast as I drink. Continuing until there is nothing left, I prowl for more and just outside the door I smell another. Barging through the door I attack, tearing at his throat like a wild lion, feeling the man die at my hands as a sense of fullness overtakes me. I realize what I've done, what I'm becoming; my thoughts become clearer and I slump next to the poor soul, torn to shreds by me and me alone.

Drake walks over, giving me a kick to the side. "Done already Cas, after 30 days of not feeding and the beating you took? I expected a few more mortals to die at your hand."

Knowing that I must still play the role of repentance I respond with respect, "Yes master. If you may be so kind, though, I would like to clean up; a shower and clean clothing would be appreciated."

“I have a shower in my office, and Marci has already laid out clothing for you. Of course, there will be guards, as I still don’t trust you to not attempt an escape.”

“Of course, I understand. When will I be allowed to return home to my apartment?”

“I may allow you later today, but I will send someone to take you, as I expect to know where you are residing. I’ve also got you a cell phone so that I may contact you at all times; you also can assume there is a tracking device in it. I insist on knowing where you are and what you are doing at all times. You are now mine.”

“Yes, master.” I begin thinking of ways to evade him; he mustn’t know when I go to see my family…he can never find out they’re my family. “May I clean up now, Sir?”

“Yes, follow me. When you are done you may join us in the main area of the club.”

Drake shows me to his office and I recognize the woman, Marci, as the same one that helped to control Danika the night she was to initiate. I nod and excuse myself to the washroom. The walls are made from a frosted glass and, like the office area, the entire washroom is white. Various hygiene products from cologne, deodorant and mouthwash are all meticulously placed upon a round mirror on the counter. There’s various scents all in mini travel size containers. I assume these are for the countless guests Drake may have that use the area. A large white towel is hanging next to the glass encased shower, and I notice a dressing table has a pair of jeans and a V-neck shirt, boxer shorts, and socks all placed perfectly in the center. Under the stool of the table rests a pair of sketchers, and a black leather jacket hangs to the side.

Marci follows me. “These are for your use; please feel free to use the products and clothing available to make yourself presentable for the master.”

“Thank you.” She returns to the main office and shuts the door behind her. Through the frosted glass, I notice her sitting on the sofa across from the washroom and watching my every move. I can hear Drake excuse himself and leave the room.

Looking in the mirror I see only slight bruising remaining on my face and the swelling nearly gone. The large amount of blood I had is returning my rapid healing and it is almost complete. I feel myself returning to my normal state of mind, and the realization of what I just did sinks in. I just killed two innocent people; memories of Ashley come rushing through my head and my heart. I turn the shower on and hop in, hoping to push my thoughts and feelings aside. I must get focused again; I need to learn what the Cerberus have planned for Danika and the rest of my family. These killings weren’t my fault, my curse took over, I try to convince myself.

∞ ∞ ∞

The club is jammed packed tonight…lots of mortals here too. I’m still finding it difficult to resist them, so I go up to the bar and order a shot, knowing that I can’t handle a tap. If I start drinking from someone again I won’t stop. It’s taking every ounce of willpower I have to resist them tonight. I notice Cyrus walking towards me.

“Cyrus, it’s good to be back in the land of the living and ever after.”

“Well, I must say Cas, I hope you’ve learned your lesson and you won’t defy us again.”

"Of course, I'll be honorable and follow you. Please accept my apologies again."

"You've paid your dues; but if it ever happens again, you will not be given a second chance. I will destroy you myself."

"Of course, I'd expect nothing less from you."

"Now enjoy yourself tonight; we will be watching you." He turns on his heel and walks away.

I mingle with the other members of the club, doing my best to avoid excessive contact with the mortals. Feeling a tap on my shoulder, I turn to see Isaac. He looks different; a disguise but still him.

In a near whisper, I greet him. "Isaac, how are you brother?"

"Good, now that I know you're okay."

"What are you doing here? It's not safe for you. No one else is with you, are they?"

"No, just me and Eliza here. We thought it would be more believable if I brought a minion."

I look over his shoulder and notice the young, tall woman I met only a few times while back with my family last month. "You have to be careful here."

"It's okay, Isaac claimed me as his alone at the door, and Ebony and I did a protection spell before I left. Even if they wanted to get me, they wouldn't be able to."

I nod with understanding. "Well, I may be allowed to go to my apartment tonight. They're watching me, so you best be on your way. I'm okay now. I'll contact the family soon."

"We just had to know you're okay. It's been a month."

"I was under the club until only today, and I'll explain everything soon. Thank you for your concern, but please, I don't want anything to happen to you. You must leave now. I promise I'll be in contact soon." I walk past the two as I don't want to raise suspicions if I'm caught talking to a new club goer for too long.

As I work the crowd I notice Isaac and Eliza hit the dance floor for a bit and the bar for a drink before they leave. I continue to mingle as I sense Drake and Cyrus watching me, and I've already identified their spy's or guards.

∞ ∞ ∞

Finally arriving at my apartment after I'm released from Club VC, just before sunset. I head straight to my journal; I must destroy all my notes. Taking a garbage can I begin to rip the pages from the book, once I find a pack of matches in my junk drawer. Striking the match, the swooshing of the flames and the smell from the burning stick remind me of times camping with the rest of the Pierce family. I toss the match in the can and watch all my notes and memories go up in flames. I know this must be done; with the Cerberus leaders watching me so closely and guards following me, they now know where I live and that they'll have someone search my apartment. I need to remove and destroy anything and everything that ties me to the Pierce family. My vampire family is on the Cerberus's radar now; after the fight and losing so many of their new members, Drake and Cyrus are out for revenge. Drake stumbled upon Danika when he was scouting the magical powers of the area. He knew then he wanted her to be his queen. I know this fight isn't over and they will be back for Danika and for my family. I go through my place with great speed, gathering anything that I can destroy, and throw it into the fire; the belongings I wish to keep can be taken to my family's house. I need to figure out a way to escape the guards Drake sent with me; maybe I can somehow sneak out the back if no one is out there watching me. This might take some time to plan, but I will get to the house and fill my family in.

Chapter 28

Loving Touch

Nathanial and I are able to convince his mom to let me practice my Reiki techniques on her.

"Kids, my tummy's been feeling so funny I am open to trying anything right now. I can't explain it; I'm not nauseated or in pain, it just feels like something going on. I went to the doctor earlier today and he isn't sure what is going on either. He did a pregnancy test just to make sure; of course, it was negative…I knew I wasn't. I've heard of Reiki before, so why not? I mean what can it harm?"

"Great! I'm a very good learner, Mrs. McCord, and I've been taking online classes." I fib a little. "Just lie down, close your eyes and relax, you might feel some heat radiating from my hands, but it shouldn't be too hot. I may gently touch you but if at any time it becomes uncomfortable just let me know," I explain.

Mrs. McCord follows my instructions and once she relaxes, I begin to complete the healing process. I can feel the healing; it's nearing completion. I feel her uterus and ovaries repairing beneath my hands. Since moving to Wenham my ability to heal has been tested to help people I care about more than it has in the last hundred years. On the sofa, Mrs. McCord is nearly asleep when Mr. McCord walks in.

"Hey kids, what are you doing to Nikole?"

"Sophia's just trying a relaxation technique she's learning to help mom with her stomach problems," Nathanial covers for me.

"I think I'm done…she's sound asleep. Why don't Nate and I fix dinner, and you can go shower while she rests," I suggest.

"Nate, you've found yourself one heck of a girl here; I suggest you keep her." He pats his son on the back as he begins to leave the room.

"Hey Dad," Nathanial hollers and his dad pauses to look over at his son. "Just want you to know that I have no plans on letting her go." He wraps his arms around my waist, sending those wonderful firework sensations off within me. His dad smiles and heads straight to the washroom.

"You know, Nate there's been so much going on we haven't really enjoyed one another in a while."

"Is that a proposition?" he kisses my neck.

"Get your mind out of the gutter, your parents are right here. I only meant that we've been preoccupied by so much we haven't had the chance to just relax and enjoy spending time together. You know all the little things."

"Yeah I get it, even when we're alone, there's still so much on our minds we haven't been able to just chill."

"Well, tonight I want you to come back to my place; that way we can do just that, and maybe a little more," I wink at the handsome man standing before me.

"But aren't you still worried about Caspian?"

"Of course, but I have to trust in the information we have and hope he returns soon." I attempt my tough girl facade.

"I'll accept this but know that I don't fully believe you." Wrapping me in a tight squeeze, Nathanial holds me close. I feel his heart beat against my chest and I melt into his arms.

With a slight touch of his hand, Nathanial lifts my chin so that our lips meet. A soft and gentle kiss turns into a deep passionate one. Moving his hands down my back and cupping my butt, he lifts me onto the kitchen counter. Slowly moving his kisses down my neck to my collarbone, it's difficult to resist, but I withdraw and push him back.

"Nate my love, your parents are right here, and I offered to cook. If we don't stop now, I don't think either one of us will have the willpower to do so. Let's make dinner and we can enjoy our alone time later tonight."

He nods and pulls back from me only to take a seat at the table for a moment. I go to the fridge and begin to pull ingredients from the shelves and prepare dinner. Once everything is ready and Mr. McCord comes out of the shower, he wakes Nathanial's mom and they both join us in the kitchen.

"Are you feeling better Nikole?" he questions.

"Now that you mention it, I am. I think your little trick there worked Sophia…thank you."

"Anything I can do to help. Your family means so much to me. I've been really worried about you."

"That's very kind of you. I feel like a new woman! I can't believe how much energy I have, and the funny feeling in my stomach is gone. Now enough fussing over me, let's enjoy dinner. Thank you for taking care of this for me while I rested Sophia. Your parents have done a great job with you, and I'm very happy Nate's brought you into our lives."

I'm humbled by her comments; I'm the lucky one to have finally found my other half; to have Nathanial in my life means more to me than anyone could ever imagine. Nathanial and I decide it might also be a good time to discuss the option of working for my family, bringing it up in a manner that make Nathanial's dad unaware that it is a job created for him. We engage in normal dinner time conversation.

"My family has some major renovations planned, so once my father and Uncle Isaac find a contractor I may need to hang out here a little more if you don't mind," I say to begin the conversation.

Nathanial's father raises his eyebrow with interest. "I can probably help out with that Sophia. I mean, if your family needs a contractor, I can go look at the job and give them a quote. Also, if it is something I can't do, I can recommend someone for them."

"Really?" I act surprised. "I know my family would be so grateful. Are you sure you have time to come look and don't mind? We've been here less than a year and still don't know all the places to go and people to talk to when we're in need of service."

"Not a problem; things are a little slow for me right now, so I have the time to help out. It's perfect. Maybe I can stop by tomorrow and talk with them."

"I'll let them know tonight that you'll be there in the morning…thank you so much."

I can't believe how easy that was; I'll let my family know when I get home a little later. Today has been such a great day; I can't imagine anything making it any better.

∞ ∞ ∞

Nathanial parks out front of the house and walks around the car to open my door for me; he really is a gentleman. Even after several months of dating, he still treats me like the very first day we met. We walk up the marble stairs to the veranda and through the large double doors of my house. This house still amazes me; this grand foyer and the large split spiral staircase is magnificent. Nathanial and I both hear laughs and talking from the family room, and hand in hand we go to see what all the commotion is about.

Sitting there on the sofa is Caspian and the rest of the family gathered around him.

"Oh my God, you're back!" I run over and hug my brother. "Why didn't you guys call me? I would've been home sooner.

"Calm down little girl, I just got here," Caspian teases.

Nathanial and I take a seat and we all inquire about what's happened in the past month. The next several hours are spent rehashing what Caspian's gone through at the hands of the Cerberus. He still has no new information, and I can't believe the torture he's endured to protect us. From what he's saying there are no plans, as of yet, of retaliation on the Cerberus' part, so I guess we can relax a little. Caspian will remain within the Cerberus' inner circle until we can plan to take them down. Elijah will contact the Renata again and try to come up with a strategy; otherwise, we just have to be prepared at all times. For tonight, we can celebrate Caspian coming back to us again. I have to admit I was a little concerned that he wouldn't come back again. Thank God he did; we need him as part of this family unit. Now we're one step closer to being complete.

"They have a tail on me. I had to sneak over here, and even though I don't think they saw me leave, I ran through the woods and made some evasive moves to lose anyone who could've been on my tail."

"So, what are you going to do now?" Constance asks.

"I have to go back. I don't have much information and I need to gather more Intel about what their plans are. We need to stop the Cerberus, and we can't do it without the inside scoop of what they have planned. I think they might want to return here for Danika, but this is the kind of thing I can find out from the inside if I prove I'm worthy to them."

"Are you kidding me? After the torture, you endured you want to go back to them?" I jump up.

Nathanial grabs me, pulling me back down into his lap. "I know you don't like this sweetie, but Caspian's right; we need to have more information to stop them. This is the best way to prevent more mortals from being Embraced."

Slumping down in his lap I concede, knowing they're right…even if I don't like it.

Chapter 29

School's Out

It's hard to believe we're finished the school year here in Wenham. We haven't had any more incidents with the Cerberus, which is a good thing. We kinda expected Drake to come back to the school for Danika, but now that it's the last day and we haven't seen him, we can't help but wonder if he believes she is still on the run from her family, from us. Caspian hasn't heard anything about her either. They've allowed him closer into the Cerberus organization if you can call it that. The Renata's requested that we keep them informed on the whereabouts and doings of the cult, but we've nothing to report.

Alexander, Matilda, Danika and I walked through these doors nearly ten months ago; Danika and I were at each other's throats, and I resented her for everything. Today we walk in not only friends but sisters, and I'm grateful that I had to come to this school. This is where I met the man of my dreams; my soul mate, and I couldn't ask for more. Danika has brought so much to our family…it's because of her that we have found a place we can call home, friends that we can trust, more people we consider like family, and our brother was brought back to us. This has been one of those full circle moments for me.

The students of Wenham High are congregated in the hallway signing yearbooks and wishing others well. Many of the seniors will be off to college in the fall.

"Hey, Sophia, will you sign my yearbook for me?" A little brunette asks.

I recognize her from the New Year's party but can't remember her name. We've had such a crazy year I didn't really didn't get to know many of the students. Maybe next year I can get to know them better, actually, give them a chance.

"Sure," I respond with a smile and write the typical thanks for a great year in her book.

Ebony, Matt, and Nathanial show up a few minutes after us, and we all clean out our lockers, sign a few more yearbooks, and prepare for the big water fight; seniors against the rest of the school. They are more than outnumbered, but I've heard this is a tradition to see the seniors off. I think it'll be so much fun, but I may have to peg Mel with a good balloon or ten. Our little close-knit group of friends volunteered to make and set up the water balloons; others are filling water guns and large buckets of water for dunking others into. A few of us have thought about tossing a couple of the teachers in there. The school is also providing a large picnic/barbeque lunch for the entire student body. This kind of thing doesn't happen in the big city.

"Hey sweetie, are you gonna be mad and kick my butt if I throw you in the dunk tank?" Nathanial nudges me.

"Yeah, as if you could."

"I think I have a pretty good chance; you can't do anything to fight me off in front of everyone. They would get pretty suspicious if a tiny little girl like you fought off a six-foot-four quarterback," he chuckles.

"Yeah, I guess so, but remember I can move so fast they wouldn't even notice what is happening. they'll just be assumed that you tripped and fell in." I smile back, shooting him a devious look.

Sticking out his tongue, Nathanial stomps and turns on the heel of his yellow DC shoes; why he loves these goofy skater shoes beats me. I can't help but laugh thinking he looks just like a toddler. He walks away to fill a few more balloons and I grab one, tossing it at him, hitting him right in between the shoulder blades.

"You did not just do that? You're going to pay now," he laughs, spinning back around and breaking into a run.

Thinking he can never catch me, I wiggle a little and make a face before I start to run away.

Alexander grabs me from the side. "Got her for you, bro," he shouts.

Nathanial comes running over, grabbing one of the buckets we're using for the balloons. As he fills it with water, I try to squirm loose from Alexander's grasp. With a squeal, Nathanial dumps the bucket not only over me but over Alexander as well.

"Seriously, I try to help you and you nail me too. Now you got two vampires against you."

Nathanial breaks into a sprint across the field from the supply room we're using and we both chase after him, not too fast as others are around. I can hear Ebony and Matt killing themselves with laughter as Danika and Matilda watch from the side. Once again, I get to experience the perfect normal moment. Finally catching Nathanial, I trip him to the ground and jump on top of him, shaking my wet hair over him like a wet dog. We're all laughing so hard, we know the chase is over. Nathanial pulls me down closer to him and moves in for a kiss. Pressing my body down on top of him, our lips begin moving together in perfect motion. The passion growing as our kisses become deeper and deeper. Remembering we are in the middle of the school field I pull myself away, still sitting on top of him. Alexander connects his thoughts with mine, trying to give me a clue. He walks up behind me and I jump off of Nathanial. Alexander tosses a bucket of water while Nathanial lies still on the ground.

"Awww dude," Nathanial jumps up, shaking like a fish out of water, as we all kill ourselves laughing.

"Okay children, maybe we should finish these balloons for the water fight," Matilda jokes.

We fill the rest of the balloons and take them over to the so-called battlegrounds. Everything seems to be in place, so we go join in on the barbeque in the school courtyard. No one notices that my siblings and I aren't in fact eating. Before long, the student body and faculty heads to the football field to commence the water activities. Of course, the seniors are demolished, as they are far outnumbered. I guess this is all part of their send off. With a skillful shot, I nail Mel in the back of the head not once, not twice, but three times. She's boiling over with anger; with each hit, I could see just a little more steam pour from her. On the third shot, Mel finally bursts and turns around, marching through the crowd screaming and yelling at every person in line with her.

"Was that you, you freakin' moron?"

Everyone moves out of her way, shaking their heads, and no one makes eye contact. I step forward, "Oh sorry Mel, my aim is so bad. I hope the water doesn't ruin your hairdo." I chuckle at the sight of her looking like a drowned rat.

“What the hell are you laughing at?”

“You, of course,” the crowd gasps at my forwardness.

“What did you say?”

“You seriously think no one here has the tenacity to stand up to you? Well, you are wrong, little girl. I’m so tired of how you think you run this school, and so are lots of other people. So here is a little hint for you…get over yourself.” Cheers erupt from others around me.

“I realize this is your first year here, but allow me to clue you in. I do run things around here, and anyone that believes differently pays for it.” Mel shoves in a little closer to me and tries to push me.

Without a flinch I go to push her back, ready to rip her scrawny little body to pieces. Danika jumps in front of me, “This would be considered a very bad idea, considering the entire school and faculty is watching right now.”

“Whatever.” Mel huffs and turns flipping her long wet hair over her shoulder spraying anyone in a two-foot radius. She storms all the way back to the girl’s locker room.

We all laugh at her drama queen antics. The principle walks towards me and my siblings, “Now Sophia, as much as I appreciate you putting Mel in her place, I can’t tolerate behavior like this at my school. I’ll have to ask you to sit out for the remainder of the water activities.”

“Yes sir, I understand and I’m sorry I lashed out in front of everyone.”

“I think we both know that’s not true. I also think we all know Mel needed to hear that. Let’s hope she’s a little more pleasant in the fall once she’s had time to think about her behavior this past year or so.”

Once the water fight is over, the students dry off in the sun for a bit and take their time entering the school to clean out lockers before dispersing for the day. I can't wait to see what the summer holds for us and all our supernatural and mortal friends alike. I'm thinking all the extra time can be used helping Ebony and Eliza prepare for more demon attacks like the one they had on Matt's birthday. Most of all, I hope to spend as much time as I can with Nathanial. I think Ebony and Matt have the same idea, and I know that Eliza and Luke have already begun as they took off for a week of camping.

It's kinda hard to believe life has changed so much from last summer when we moved back to Wenham. Danika and I are getting along much better; I even think I might enjoy having her around. I have found the love of my life, my soul mate and the one that completes me all wrapped up into one little package. The witch that gave us the sun, is back in our lives, along with her wonderful granddaughters and my new best friend. The Magnificent Ones are learning to use their powers for good. We even made a few friends with the shapeshifters. Then, of course, the one thing I would have never thought could happen…Caspian came back into our lives. I only hope he is doing alright with his undercover mission. Gosh, now that I really start thinking about it, all these things barely touch the iceberg of things my family and I went through this year. Let's just hope it keeps getting better and Caspian can return to us as a more permanent member of the family. I guess only time will tell…for now, we celebrate. Tomorrow we can get back to business.

∞ ∞ ∞

Mr. McCord has been working hard for several months now, renovating the house and Isaac's workspace. Helping them in whatever way I can has become such a pleasure for me and I know he takes pride in the work he's doing. With Nathanial's dad taking care of the renovations, Isaac's been able to work on his synthetic blood and has even begun to prepare the paper-work, so he can present it to the FDA, and maybe even begin the initial stages of human testing. We've started to incorporate his blood into our daily meals; it's better than the animal blood too. With a similar taste to real blood and also the ability to give us the strength of real blood, it's very enjoyable. Slowly we'll remove the donated blood that Isaac has been getting from the hospital and blood banks, testing if we can fully survive on the synthetic blood. With so much going on I have a feeling that the summer will keep us busy. I still worry about Caspian, but the Cerberus may have to be put on the back burner as we help The Magnificent Ones. The demonic activity around them has been increasing ever since the first attack on the night of Matt's birthday. I guess for now we will just have to see what the future holds.

About the Author

Charlotte Blackwell author of The Embrace Series is delighted to have the opportunity to follow her dreams of writing. She would love to share a little bit about herself with you now.

Charlotte was born in October of 1976. On the day of her birth, Charlotte's father was racing stock cars, while her two older sisters watched from the stands as their father crashed through the wall of the race track. Within moments the stock car he was driving came back through the wall, and he won the race. He took his two daughters and hurried to the hospital for the birth of his third daughter, Charlotte.

Raised in Edmonton, Alberta, Charlotte enjoyed swimming, singing (although not so great at it) and writing her thoughts down. She never shared her passion for writing with anyone, and it got put on the back burner. As Charlotte grew, she found a new passion in medicine; she became the athletic trainer for her high school men's basketball team. Helping the team through their injuries are some of her best memories as a teen.

After the birth of her first daughter Jorden, Charlotte moved to Calgary, Alberta where she returned to college for her practical nursing certificate. During her schooling, Charlotte became pregnant with her second daughter, Shawnee. Due to complications, Charlotte was put on bed rest and had to step away from school. Shawnee was born and not breathing, the staff worked to resuscitate the small baby, and succeeded. Charlotte returned to school only six weeks later and completed her course. She began working with children, and eventually in the special care nursery for ill and pre-term babies.

Charlotte and James finally decided to get married in 2005 and completed their family with a son, Lucas in 2006 who was born six weeks early and had three surgeries by one-month-old. Today all three of their children are happy, healthy and very active, Jorden is a very talented dancer and singer who lives in Las Vegas where she works and attends college. Shawnee is a competitive dancer and is working very hard. Lucas is still young but loves all things computers, including programming all before he's even a teenager.

Charlotte and James live with 2 of their children, and many animals just outside of Calgary, Alberta. They cherish every moment they have together as a family and hope to soon travel the world. James and the children have been great supporters of Charlotte from day one and continue to cheer her on along the way.

Charlotte has a strong passion for young adult novels especially those in the paranormal or dark fantasy genres. As she continues to work on The Embrace Series, Charlotte is also working on a mainstream romance. She will continue to update her site with her work and what is next, and she thanks you all for your support and encouragement.

http://charlotteblackwell.blogspot.com/

https://www.facebook.com/CharlotteBlackwellAuthor/

https://twitter.com/CharBlackwell

https://www.instagram.com/charblackwellbooks/

https://www.goodreads.com/author/dashboard

https://amazon.com/author/charblackwellbooks

Mystic Embrace

Book Three
The Embrace Series
Available August 28, 2018

91549555R10139

Made in the USA
San Bernardino, CA
25 October 2018